Lost and
Found

UNEXPECTED MAGIC – BOOK 3

CHRISTINE POPE

LOST AND FOUND

Copyright © 2022 by Christine Pope

ISBN: 978-1-946435-56-9

Published by Dark Valentine Press

Cover design by Lou Harper

Ebook formatting by Indie Author Services

Chapter 1
Riddle Me This

Ride the roan to find the patriarch's tears.
Pour out a blessing to bury one's fears.
As above, so below,
Circle of iron to cast down your foe.

The words of the poem or riddle or whatever it was that I'd found buried somewhere deep within the Sangre de Cristo mountains northeast of Taos had echoed through my mind so many times over the past week, I pretty much had them memorized by this point.

Too bad they still didn't make any damn sense. All the same, I knew they had to be crucial in some way, knew there had to be a specific reason why the patriarch's tears were mentioned in the first line of the riddle...as though I'd be doomed in my attempt to learn more about my biological mother and discover exactly why she'd left me these clues if I didn't first determine what those tears were, and why they were so important that a riddle describing them had been hidden inside a secret cave, one that only I had been able to unlock.

Isaac Zamora, my magical guide and significant other—"boyfriend" felt like such a silly word to apply to a grown man of thirty-six, especially one with Isaac's *gravitas*—hadn't been able to puzzle out their meaning, either. However, he'd only told me we'd figure it out in time, but for now, we might as well focus on other things.

Namely, the sword I'd found inside the mountain, the one that apparently had a unique magical gift for demon-slaying.

In all his research, Isaac so far hadn't been able to find a single reference to such a weapon. That didn't necessarily mean much, since even with my brief acquaintance with magic and all the havoc it could cause, I could tell that magical lore wasn't something which had exactly been codified and standardized to make life easier for workers of magic. Each family seemed to have its own brand of enchantments, and, while Isaac had inherited his witch mother's grimoire and her abilities, along with the house where he lived and the store in Santa Fe's downtown that sold various woo-woo items, there was definitely nothing in her spell book which mentioned an enchanted sword that killed demons, rather than simply banishing them.

"There's always the possibility that your biological mother made the sword," he remarked as we sat in front of the fire in his living room on a chilly November night and discussed the problematic weapon.

I frowned. "That doesn't seem very likely."

He shrugged and reached for his glass of wine. Expression thoughtful, he sipped some tempranillo before replying, "It's hard to say, since we don't know anything about her abilities, other than she was a lodestone like you."

A lodestone was a witch who attracted magical items to her, just like metal filings to a magnet. I'd found out about being a lodestone the hard way, by attracting a pair of enchanted eyeglasses to me that revealed the place of my biological mother's death, a lonely canyon with red rock walls looming on either side. Since red rock canyons weren't exactly in short supply in this part of the world, it definitely wouldn't be an easy task to try to figure out the exact location where her body had been buried, in a shallow grave scratched out by the demon who'd killed her.

Since Isaac had sent that same demon back to hell a month earlier, we wouldn't have the opportunity to pick his brain on the subject. Not that we probably would have gotten the answers we wanted; the demon had been chatty enough about certain topics, but it seemed clear to me during our little face-off that he wasn't about to reveal anything involving my bio-mom's identity, or the identity of her own mother, a murderous witch who'd sent the demon to murder her daughter for her disobedience.

"Anyway," Isaac went on, since I continued to stare into the fireplace, brooding over all the things I didn't know about the woman who'd given me her flaming red hair and cool gray eyes, "if she was a strong enough witch to hide the key to the secret chamber inside a rock wall and then cast an enchantment to conceal the sword and the riddle deep in the mountains, then it's not outside the bounds of possibility that she might also have been strong enough to create a sword with the specific purpose of killing demons." He paused there, fingers tapping against the stem of his wine glass as he pondered the conundrum. "She wouldn't have necessarily had to forge the sword itself. Maybe she took an ordinary sword and bound it with enchantments to create its demon-killing properties."

That theory felt a little more plausible to me. The sword was a beautiful little thing, smaller than an ordinary longsword but bigger than a dagger, something that felt perfectly balanced in my hand. In fact, the hilt fit my fingers perfectly, almost as though it had been made for me. But what if it hadn't been custom made, but was something my biological mother had chosen because she'd known if it fit her hand, it would fit mine as well?

Of course, if that's really what had happened, then it would seem to indicate she'd known one of the eggs she'd donated some thirty-odd years ago would be used to create a daughter, someone who would have her powers. According to Isaac, magical gifts were passed from mother to daughter somewhere around half the time, while *brujos*—male witches—were far, far rarer.

And yes, it seemed I'd been conceived from a donated egg. I hadn't learned the truth about that fun little fact until a month ago, although it definitely explained why I didn't look anything like the woman who'd raised me, and why she'd always shown a thinly veiled—or sometimes not veiled at all—hostility toward her only daughter. For whatever reason, she'd never been able to bond with the child she'd carried all those months. If it weren't for my father and his obvious affection for me, my childhood would have been a lot rougher than it already had been.

Sure, some people probably would have rolled their eyes at my supposed sob story—*look at the poor little rich girl*—but money couldn't fix all problems, and it definitely hadn't been able to make my mother love me the way a mother was supposed to love her child.

"Well, whatever my bio-mom did, it was obviously effective," I replied, and drank some of my own tempranillo. We hadn't quite finished the bottle from dinner, and that was why we'd decided to take the remnants into the living room so we could enjoy the fire there. "Because that demon was deader than a doornail."

And had left a messy corpse on my bedroom floor. Luckily, Isaac had thought to sprinkle the body with holy water, and it had basically evaporated into nothing, saving us from having to dispose of the dead demon in a landfill or something.

Isaac nodded. He had his hands wrapped around his wine glass as though trying to warm its contents, although he seemed satisfied for the moment to merely hold it rather than trying to drink any of the tempranillo inside. "It's very powerful magic that can kill a being that's supposed to be immortal," he said. "And a very good weapon to have in your arsenal."

"Definitely," I agreed. Maybe I'd never be able to figure out the crazy riddle my biological mother had left behind, but at least the sword she'd given me had already proven its effectiveness.

Killing the demon had been pretty much dumb luck. Or rather, I'd lunged and taken the unholy creature by surprise, running him through with the sword before he had a chance to react. However, since Isaac had determined that I shouldn't keep going on serendipity alone, he'd found someone to teach me the basics of sword fighting.

After being with him for more than a month, I wasn't as surprised by the way he'd been able to dig up a sword fighting tutor as I might have been. I'd already known he'd once been fairly active in the Society for Creative Anachronism, a medieval reen-actment group, and so it just made sense that he had someone in his circle who could teach me the basics.

True, most of the fighting in the SCA was done with fake weapons—pieces of rattan wrapped in duct tape to mimic everything from massive two-handed broadswords to axes and maces—but they also had a group that worked with live steel, mainly for demos and other educational opportunities. My teacher in sword-craft, Tim O'Neil, was a tall, thin guy with lightning reflexes and what appeared to be infinite patience with my beginner clumsiness. I could only hope that under his tutelage, I'd be able to successfully kill any other demons dumb enough to cross my path.

Not, of course, that we'd told Tim I was trying to hone my skills as a demon slayer. No, Isaac had concocted a story about how I was an actress who would be auditioning for a part in some fantasy ripoff B-grade movie, and I needed to be able to handle a sword believably on-screen.

Never mind that the mere notion of appearing in front of a camera, when I'd spent most of my professional life behind the scenes as a prop shopper, was enough to make me break out in hives.

"It's like my bio-mom knew the demons would be coming after me," I said, and Isaac gave a grave nod, his expression troubled.

"It does feel that way," he replied. "I suppose if she knew her own mother would seek revenge for her daughter's disobedience, then she also wouldn't hesitate to go after her granddaughter as well."

At least, that was what the first demon had more or less told me—that once my powers had started to blossom after my arrival in New Mexico, I'd suddenly appeared on that scary witch's radar, and she'd decided it was time to bring me into the fold.

A fate I was doing my damnedest to avoid. My own family was dysfunctional enough, but I had a feeling my biological grandmother would make them look like the Tanners from *Full House.*

"Well, she can try," I said, the words much bolder than I actually felt. I glanced toward the coat closet, where the sword was propped up against one wall. Hidden from view, but I knew it was there. Despite my rented home's more than adequate security system, I didn't feel comfortable leaving something so valuable behind, and so I brought it with me pretty much everywhere I went.

Isaac laid a hand on mine, warm, strong. Even though we'd been seeing one another for more than a month, we still hadn't done much more than kiss, and so by that point, even the slightest touch from him was enough to send my blood racing. I kept telling myself over and over that I needed to wait until he felt comfortable being intimate, that the accident which had nearly killed him and confined him to a wheelchair for several years...even though he mostly got around on crutches now and could even walk unassisted if he didn't push too hard... had made him hesitant, unsure whether he was ready to take that next step between us. Somewhere deep inside, I knew he'd be worth waiting for.

Good words, and the truth. All the same, I had to wonder how much longer I could endure this forced celibacy.

"Yes, she can try," he said, echoing my words. "But I don't think she'll be successful."

The trees in my yard were now almost bare, even though we were only a week into November. But the skies above Santa Fe were as brightly blue as ever, and I couldn't help feeling cheerful when I got up the next morning after my dinner with Isaac and started getting ready for my day. Yes, I'd been fired back at the end of September from my job as a prop shopper after being heinously late on set twice in a row, but I'd managed to land on my feet. Isaac had gotten me in touch with an indie film producer, Peter Nielsen, who needed a storyboard artist, and he'd liked my work so much that he'd passed my info along to a director friend of his, someone who'd turned around and hired me right away after I'd wrapped up the project for Peter.

If the jobs kept flowing like this, I definitely wouldn't have to worry about supporting myself. Yes, there might be dry spells here and there, but my father had given me a large cash cushion when my ex, Dave Zelinsky, and I broke up, and I'd barely touched the capital.

And true, after Dave had dropped dead in my living room, the victim of a heart attack brought on by a demon revealing itself to him in all its awful glory, I knew I'd also be receiving survivor benefits from the Rancho Cucamonga police department... not to mention the payout from a hefty life insurance policy...but I'd already resolved not to touch those funds except in the direst of circumstances. I'd donated about half of what I'd receive in survivor benefits to my former best friend and Dave's baby mama, Casey McMasters, partly out of misplaced guilt, and partly because some part of me truly believed she would have married him just as soon as he got our divorce papers properly filed, and therefore those benefits should have been hers.

All had been quiet on the Southern California front lately, for which I was eternally grateful. Now that it was clear I wouldn't be trying to get my claws on any of the equity in Dave's house and wanted nothing more than to have that whole mess completely out of my life, my former in-laws had pretty much left me alone. I had no doubt another battle would erupt whenever the insurance company finally coughed up the payout on his policy, but I was just fine with putting off that evil day for as long as possible.

It was a quiet morning of work interrupted by a brief lunch, followed by an equally quiet after-noon. I knew Isaac was working at the store that Monday, and since he had a private client afterward for some kind of spell work, we wouldn't be getting together for dinner. And I tried to tell myself that was fine—we'd been together just the evening before, and he was planning to come over Tuesday night after work.

Still, I missed him. Not for the first time, I told myself not to be clingy, that we were now routinely seeing each other at least three or four times a week, which felt like a lot considering we'd only been dating—or whatever you wanted to call what we were doing—for about a month. All the same, I wasn't really looking forward to spending the evening alone.

A little before five, someone knocked at the door, and I laid down my pencil, frowning slightly. While it wasn't unheard-of to get unexpected visitors in my neighborhood, anything from kids selling candy for school fundraisers to people canvassing for the latest municipal election, it wasn't exactly common, either.

And after having demons show up on my doorstep several times in a row, I could probably be forgiven for being a bit gun-shy.

For just a second, I wondered if I should ignore the knock. Then I reminded myself that my house was protected by ward piled upon ward, that the protection candle Isaac and I had made together still burned steadily on the peninsula in the kitchen, and that I also wore an amulet he'd given me as an extra layer of defense against dark magic and/or demon intrusion. No one who harbored any ill will toward me would have been able to cross the property line at all, let alone make it all the way up the front walk to the door.

So I got up from my chair and went to the door, wishing the fall wreath I'd hung a few days earlier didn't do such a good job of covering up the peephole. Since that obvious failing couldn't be helped now, I didn't have much choice except to open the door and hope for the best.

About the last person I would have expected to see stood there, a half smile on his lips and a glint of amusement in his blue eyes.

"Hi, Penny," my father said. "Mind if I come in?"

Chapter 2
Loose Ends

"D ad?" I said in incredulous tones.

"I know this is a little unexpected," he said, casual as though he'd just dropped by on his way to the golf course.

Just a little, I thought. All the same, I replied quickly, "No, it's great to see you. Come on in."

I stepped out of the way so he could enter the house. Luckily, I'd performed my Sunday ritual of tidying up and wiping down all the surfaces just the day before, so besides the easel I'd set up in the living room where I could catch the afternoon light, everything was in order, the place looking warm and mellow as the sun began to make its way toward the horizon.

He sent an approving glance around, clearly glad that I'd landed in such upscale surroundings.

The house was definitely Southwest in style, with its beamed ceilings and wooden floors, and very different from the coldly elegant midcentury-modern house where I'd grown up and where he and my mother still lived, but it seemed obvious to me that he liked what he saw.

"Can I get you anything?" I asked. "Water? Tea? A glass of wine?"

I'd been half-joking when I offered the wine, but he took me seriously. "Water is fine."

"Just a sec," I told him. "Go ahead and sit wherever you like."

My father settled himself on the couch, and I hurried into the kitchen to freshen the glass of water I'd poured for myself an hour earlier and to fetch a new glass for him. When I returned to the living room, I noticed at once that he'd set an envelope down on the coffee table.

"What's that?" I inquired as I handed him the glass of water, then sat down on the couch across from him.

His gaze followed mine to the envelope where it rested on the table. "It's the check from the insurance company. I guess they sent it to the house by mistake rather than to your box here in Santa Fe."

Typical. I couldn't help noticing that the envelope had been opened. Probably, Casey had pounced as soon as she saw who the letter was from...only to have her hopes dashed as she realized the cashier's check was made out to me and she couldn't do a damn thing with it. No one could accuse her of making the best life choices, but I guessed even she had realized trying to forge my signature and depositing the check in her own account was a bridge too far.

"So, you came all the way to Santa Fe just to deliver a letter?" I said, smiling a little despite myself.

However, my father's expression remained serious. As always, he looked casually elegant, his gray-salted light brown hair cut close, his lean, handsome face sporting a slight tan. He drank some of the water I'd brought him, then replied, "Well, it's a big chunk of money. I could have couriered it, I suppose, but I also wanted to talk to you in person."

That didn't sound good. He looked solemn enough, but I couldn't detect any real tension in him, no sign that he'd also traveled here because he needed to tell me face to face that he'd been diagnosed with cancer or something equally dire.

"About...?" I said, doing my best to ignore the quiver in my stomach. True, my father didn't seem particularly worried or on edge, but I couldn't quite believe he would have come all this way just to pay his only daughter a visit.

He leaned forward slightly. As usual when he

didn't have to go to a meeting or some other quasi-formal occasion, he had on expensive dress slacks and a dress shirt, but no tie or jacket. And he didn't have that slightly weary air most people tended to wear after enduring a commercial flight, leading me to believe he'd chartered a plane to fly him straight to Santa Fe. Unlike a lot of his friends, he didn't own a plane, but he did make casual use of expensive charter flights the way some people would call an Uber.

"I was going to talk to you about it at Dave's funeral," my father said. "But then you left so quickly, and I decided I might as well wait to broach the subject until I had something concrete to give you. It might have all been a wild-goose chase in the end."

"*What* would have been a wild-goose chase?" I demanded. Maybe I should have tried a little harder to temper my tone, but his oblique references were only setting me more on edge.

He drank some more water, then set down the glass. "I hired a private investigator to look into the fertility clinic where your mother and I got our donor egg."

About all I could do was blink at him. Yes, he'd told me only a month earlier that he and my mother had used an egg donor to conceive me, and he'd also told me that the doctor who'd performed the procedure had retired soon afterward and shut down his clinic. Since all those records had been sealed more than thirty years earlier, not long after I was born, I hadn't thought there was much else we could do in terms of using that angle to unearth my biological mother's identity.

But apparently, my father hadn't been of the same opinion.

"And?" I asked. "Did you find anything about her?"

He didn't bother to ask who I meant by "her." "Not exactly," he said. "That is, Dr. Lightman got the donor eggs from another clinic, one in Albuquerque. The eggs were identified by control numbers, not names, in order to keep the donors anonymous. But the private investigator was able to learn that your biological mother donated five eggs in total. Three were disposed of when Dr. Lightman retired and the clinic was closed down. One was you, of course"—my father paused there to smile briefly—"and the last one was given to another of Dr. Lightman's patients. She had a son about eight months after you were born."

About all I could do was blink at this unexpected piece of information. Yes, I'd wondered whether I had any half-siblings out there I hadn't known about...and had worried that they might also become targets for my mysterious, murderous witch grandmother...but because I hadn't known how I could possibly track them down, I'd thought they'd have to remain a mystery to me.

"So...I have another half-brother?" I asked. It still felt strange to think of my little brother Cade in that way, since for the vast majority of my life, he'd just been my brother and nothing else. But, biologically speaking, we were only half-siblings.

My father's smile disappeared. "Well, you *did* have another half-brother. He was born in Los Angeles, like you were, but he'd recently relocated to Denver for his work." A heavy pause, as if he really didn't want to continue, but then he said, "He passed away about six months ago."

For a long moment, I just stared back at my father, not sure how I was supposed to react to such a bombshell. Then I found my voice and said, "Do you know how he died?"

Another of those weighty pauses. He shifted on the couch so he moved backward slightly, his back now touching the sofa cushions. "A heart attack out of nowhere, is what the P.I. told me."

A trickle of cold moved down my spine, even as I thought, *Oh, like that isn't fishy at all.*

I knew unexpected fatalities happened all the time, and yet, after having my ex-husband drop dead of a heart attack thanks to demonic interference, I wasn't for a second going to believe this newfound half-brother of mine had died a natural death.

Problem was, my father didn't know anything about what had really caused Dave's heart attack, and I wanted to keep it that way. He could think what he wanted about how I'd decided to stay in New Mexico, despite losing the job that had been my only reason for relocating here. Luckily, he'd never been the sort of parent who'd expected me to justify all my decisions to him...quite unlike my mother. But if I tried to tell him I'd recently learned I was a witch who'd inherited some crazy gifts from my egg-donor bio-mom, and that the guy I was dating was a *brujo* who was doing his best to guide me through the awakening of those powers, he'd probably think I was having an early midlife crisis and try to hustle me back to California so I could get professional help.

And that didn't even include telling him about magic compasses and demon-killing swords hidden deep inside mountains. Those sorts of stories definitely would have made me sound like a candidate for the rubber room.

"That's...odd," I managed at last, even as I did my best to ignore an odd little pang that twinged somewhere deep inside me, a stab of loss for someone I'd never known. What had he been like, this half-brother of mine? Had he been a redhead, too, or had he taken after his father? Had he been tall, or short? Smart and friendly, or sort of a jerk?

My father picked up his glass and drank some

more water. "I thought so, too, especially considering what happened to Dave." A very small shake
of his head, as though he'd taken that moment to
contemplate all the weird synchronicities the world
threw at us, and then he went on, "But the private
investigator said he checked the police reports, and
it looked to be natural causes. The man died in his
sleep."

Well, I supposed there were worse ways to go.
All the same, none of this felt right to me. "Any
family?" I asked. Maybe I'd never be able to meet
this half-brother, but it was possible I had some
nieces and nephews out there.

However, that hope was also dashed as my
father said, "He was married, but they didn't have
any kids. His wife moved back to California after
his death."

So much for that idea. I slumped against the
back of the couch, not sure how I should respond
to the unwelcome information I'd just received.

"I'm sorry," my father said quietly. "I wish I
had better news to tell you. But the P.I. did give me
this."

He pulled his phone out of his pocket, then
opened the Photos app and handed the phone over
to me. Looking down, I saw an image of a man
around thirty, with brown hair and gray eyes that
appeared to be almost the same shade as mine.
Otherwise, I couldn't detect much of a resem-

blance between the two of us, other than a quirk at the corner of his mouth that seemed to imply his smile might be shaped almost like my own.

"What was his name?" I asked, even though I knew that particular piece of information probably wouldn't matter in the end. He would have had his parents' last name, nothing that might connect him to the woman who'd given both of us her clear gray eyes. Still, I felt as though knowing his name would at least make me feel as if I'd known him a little better.

"Luke Jackson," my father replied at once. "The P.I. told me his family lives in Thousand Oaks. He had a younger sister who was also apparently born from a donor egg. Not your biological mother's, though," he added quickly, as though he wanted to make sure his words wouldn't arouse any false hope in me.

Well, he'd already told me earlier that my mother had donated five eggs and only two of them had been used, so I'd realized at once that Luke Jackson's younger sister and I couldn't be related. I released a breath and said, "Thanks for finding all this out. Did your investigator locate any evidence that my bio-mom might have donated more of her eggs to a different clinic?"

"No," my father replied. "That is, I suppose it's possible, since he was only able to trace her donation back to the original clinic in Albuquerque, but even if she did, that would be almost impossible to track down. We don't have a starting point to work with like we did with Dr. Lightman's clinic in L.A."

Right. I supposed I should have thought of that. Even as I'd asked the question, though, something in my bones told me she hadn't gone around the country donating eggs whenever she got short on cash, but had gone to the Albuquerque clinic in desperation and done what she needed to do, then fled again. The demon who'd killed her must have caught up with her some time later, but exactly how much later? Weeks? Months?

It was impossible to know for sure. About all I could do was keep trying to unravel the mystery she'd left behind. Had she realized she was doomed, and, knowing she didn't have the time to carry a child of her own to term, had donated her eggs in a desperate attempt to leave behind an heir who might be able to stand up to the woman who'd had her killed?

Maybe. If that was the case, though, I hoped her faith in her future heirs hadn't been entirely misplaced. True, Isaac and I had banished one demon, and I'd managed to kill one entirely on my own, but I still didn't know whether I was up to the task of confronting a much older witch with powers I couldn't begin to imagine. Honestly, if I was some kind of chosen one, I couldn't help thinking I'd gotten a very late start. Someone like Isaac, who'd been trained to use his powers from the moment they began to develop, would have a much better chance than a woman like me, who'd only stumbled into her unexpected gifts a month earlier and didn't have a very good grasp of what exactly she was supposed to do with them.

It seemed I'd been quiet for too long, because my father said, "I know this is upsetting, but I thought you should know. Or was I wrong about that?"

"No," I said at once. "Of course you needed to tell me. I'm just trying to work through all of it." I stopped there and slanted a glance over at him. "Does Mom know?"

That question got me an emphatic shake of the head. "I haven't said anything to her," my father replied. "Maybe I should have, but the time has never seemed right, and I decided it was better not to rock the boat." His mouth twitched in a rueful half smile. "I guess that's taking the coward's way out."

I could see why he might think that, even if I didn't agree with his assessment of the situation. "I don't know," I said. "I mean, she was the one who insisted on keeping this whole thing a secret from me, right? Some people might say turnabout was fair play."

Now he almost chuckled. "I suppose I can see

that," he said. "All the same, I do plan to say something to her at some point. I'm glad you're fine with me waiting, though."

"Take as long as you need," I said dryly, and once again his lips quirked, revealing a smile that looked as though he wasn't sure he should be wearing it, considering we were sharing a joke at his wife's expense.

Then his gaze moved toward the envelope lying on the coffee table. "Are you going to look at that?"

I really would have preferred not to, but since my father had brought the thing all this way, it did seem kind of rude not to open it. Without replying, I leaned forward and picked up the envelope, then slid out the check inside. I'd already known that Dave's life insurance policy was for half a million dollars, but still, it was unsettling to have all those zeroes staring back at me.

For an uncomfortable moment, I only held the check in one hand as I gazed down at it. Then, without saying anything, I put it and its accompanying envelope down on the table.

"You're going to keep it," my father said, his tone firm, and I stared back at him in surprise.

"I don't think I should."

"Well, I do." He stopped there to fortify himself with a sip of water before continuing. "I know what you did for Casey's GoFundMe, and I think that's more than enough."

I didn't bother to ask how he'd figured out I was the one who'd forked over that twenty-five grand, despite the way I'd made sure the donation would be anonymous. There wasn't anyone else in my former circle who had that kind of money lying around, and my father knew me well enough to guess I'd made the gesture out of misplaced guilt and not because I owed Casey McMasters a damn thing.

Rather than contradict him directly, I said, "Dad, she's got a baby on the way, and I don't think Dave's parents can afford to pay the mortgage on the house and on their own place for very long."

"There is no mortgage," he told me, and I blinked at him.

"What?"

Our house payments had been high because Dave had gotten a fifteen-year mortgage on the place. We had about six years left paying on it, and, back before our marriage had fractured into a thousand pieces, he liked to wax rhapsodic about how much spare cash we'd have after the house was paid off, had made comments about maybe getting a boat or a condo in Arizona, something that would justify all the scrimping and saving. Anyway, because I'd seen the mortgage statements for myself, I knew exactly how much was left on the loan.

My father set down his water glass and said calmly, "I paid it off."

That statement came from so far out in left field, I didn't know how to react. "You *what?*" I blurted.

Now he was wearing his poker face, the expression that had served him in good stead over years of hard negotiating during various real estate deals. "I paid the remaining balance and told the Zelinskys that they could do what they wanted with the house after this, but that they needed to leave you alone about the life insurance money and the survivor benefits. If Dave hadn't made such a hash of things by not getting the divorce finalized when he was supposed to, then you wouldn't have been his beneficiary, and that money would have gone to his family."

All of those statements were nothing more than the cold, hard truth, even if I wasn't sure I wanted to admit it to myself. "How did they react?"

"Well, I could tell Ramona wanted to argue with me," my father said easily. "But Howard talked her down. He probably realized that I could take back my offer if they decided to be difficult, so they accepted the money. Whether they plan to let Casey live there rent-free indefinitely is their problem, but now at least all they need to worry about are the property taxes."

Property taxes that could easily be covered by the money Casey had raised in her GoFundMe. All the same, I felt as though I should offer at least a token protest. "Dad, that's a lot of money."

He shrugged. "It was a lot less than what you got from the insurance company, not to mention those survivor benefits." Fixing me with a stern blue gaze, he added, "All the same, it would probably be better if you avoided any further stunts like that one you pulled with Casey's fundraiser. You need to have that money coming in since your employment is so up in the air right now."

"I already have another storyboard gig lined up," I told him, feeling a bit wounded that he didn't think I'd be able to support myself without those benefits coming in.

"Good," he said. "And you're probably going to do just fine. All the same, it never hurts to have a cushion."

One would think the cushion he'd already provided for me—not to mention that big fat check from the life insurance company—would be enough to ensure I wouldn't be out on the street any time soon. But because I could tell he was concerned, I didn't try to argue the point. If the past month had taught me anything, it was that sometimes life could throw you some serious curveballs.

"Okay," I replied. Then, because I thought it

might be better to move on to less fraught topics, I asked, "So, where are you staying?"

"At the Turquoise Bear," he said, naming an exclusive B&B in Santa Fe's downtown. It was the sort of place that was regularly booked months in advance, so one wouldn't think he should have been able to just drop in the way he had.

However, I knew his assistant Marcy was a miracle worker when it came to that sort of thing, so no doubt she'd been able to wrangle a last-minute reservation despite the odds.

"And you're here for...?" I ventured. Not that I wasn't happy to have my father around for as long as he wanted to stay—seeing him like this had only made me realize how much I'd missed him—but if he was planning an extended trip to Santa Fe, then I'd have to make some adjustments to my schedule.

"Just today and tomorrow," he replied, now looking almost amused, as if he'd guessed all too clearly what I was thinking. "Did you have plans for tonight? I thought it would be nice to have dinner if you were free."

Well, at least I could accommodate him there, since Isaac was seeing a client and I'd been reluctantly looking forward to an evening alone. "No plans," I replied. "Where would you like to go?"

"I was thinking Geronimo," he said.

Of course my father would want to go to one of Santa Fe's most expensive restaurants—and I had no doubt he'd be able to get a reservation without any problems, even though again, it was the sort of place where you didn't just casually drop in.

No point in protesting. I smiled and said, "Geronimo would be great."

Chapter 3
Family Ties

And we did end up having a wonderful dinner. In general, you reserved a place like Geronimo for birthdays or anniversaries, but I had to admit it was sort of decadent to eat there just because we could, to dine on elk tenderloin and rack of lamb as though it was the sort of thing I did every day. After my father left the house earlier that afternoon, I'd called Isaac to let him know what was going on and to check and make sure it was all right to have my dad join us for our dinner scheduled for the following evening.

"That sounds great," he'd told me. "I'd like to meet your father."

Not a single comment about how it was too soon for that sort of thing...not that I'd really expected Isaac to make that kind of remark. I'd been a little worried he might think I was putting too much pressure on our nascent relationship, but clearly, he didn't feel that way. No, he only told me he was looking forward to it, and that had been the end of the discussion.

My father left around four, which gave me just enough time to go to the bank and deposit the cashier's check from the insurance company. Once it cleared, I'd start moving the money around so none of my accounts would be over the federally insured limit, but at least that way I'd gotten the ball rolling.

Over dinner at Geronimo, my father asked about life in Santa Fe, and commented, "It seems to suit you. I can't remember the last time you looked this happy."

"I do?" I responded, startled. One would think that with all the demon interference and the need to learn how to use a sword and the way I had to keep refreshing the protection enchantments that encircled my house, I might have been looking a little frayed around the edges.

He answered my question with a smile, saying, "Yes, you do. Or maybe it's not the town, but this man you've been seeing?"

I had no doubt that Isaac Zamora's presence in my life had a great deal to do with my current state of well-being. At the same time, I wasn't sure I wanted to make that kind of admission so early in our relationship. "Maybe a little of both," I allowed.

It seemed my father could tell I didn't want to say much more on the subject than that, and so instead he asked whether I had any time the next day to show him around, or whether he should plan to visit the local points of interest on his own. Because I had plenty of time to finish my current storyboard project, I said I'd love to take him to visit some of my favorite places, and we agreed to have him come over late the next morning so we could go exploring.

Even as I made those plans, though, I found myself hoping I wouldn't have to worry about any kinds of supernatural shenanigans interfering with our outing. True, everything had been quiet since I skewered that demon in my bedroom a week ago on Halloween, but that didn't mean much. I'd had several weeks of peace after Isaac and I banished the first demon, but then I'd stumbled across that magical compass in the gutter on my street, and everything had gone downhill pretty quickly after that.

I told myself not to borrow trouble. I'd cast some extra protection spells before my father came over and hope that should be enough to keep us safe during the day.

And if I saw any strange objects in a gutter or

on a sidewalk, well, I'd just keep walking and wouldn't let myself pick them up.

Everything was going to be fine.

The weather definitely seemed to be cooperating the next day—bright and sunny, with just a few puffy clouds floating overhead and temperatures several degrees above normal—and that felt like a good omen to me. Because I'd already planned a crockpot meal of pot roast and veggies, I was able to perform all the food prep before my father came over and knew that even if we didn't make it back to the house until late afternoon, I'd still have plenty of time to pull everything together before Isaac was scheduled to appear at six-thirty.

The Georgia O'Keeffe Museum was my favorite, so we started there, afterward roaming in and out of several galleries before we headed over to the Santa Fe Art Museum and made the rounds of that particular institution. At the galleries, my father took several business cards and made notations on the back regarding the pieces he admired the most. With a lot of other people, that would have been a polite way of giving a gallery owner the impression of being interested without having any real intention of buying something, but my father didn't operate that way. No, he'd go back to the hotel and do some research, and then would make his decisions. I doubted any of the pieces would end up in the house—my mother would never allow him to purchase something that would hang on her walls without her express approval—but he also had a large collection displayed at his office in Beverly Hills, and I assumed any acquisitions would end up there.

We had a fabulous lunch at The Shed, where we both gorged ourselves on New Mexico–style enchiladas, served flat rather than rolled like the enchiladas I'd grown up on back home in California, and then walked around the Plaza and explored more stores, many of which specialized in antique Native American jewelry and art. My father seemed intrigued by everything, although I noticed he didn't bother to buy any pieces to take back with him as a present for my mother. Her taste ran to sparkly rocks, not turquoise, and even though some of the stores here did have some items she might have liked, I could tell he was holding back because she always preferred to pick things out for herself.

However, at one shop I found my gaze caught by a gorgeous silver necklace shaped like a pair of ravens holding an exquisite piece of spiderweb turquoise between them. I'd never seen anything like it before, and bent closer to the case to get a better look.

"You like that one?" my father asked, his tone almost eager. No doubt he was hoping he'd be able to purchase something for me, a piece that would always remind me of his trip to Santa Fe.

I almost demurred, then realized I should let him do this for me. Even though I guessed the necklace must be fairly expensive, it wasn't like I was asking him to buy the crown jewels for me or something. I'd just have to hope a day would come when I wouldn't have to wear the protection amulet Isaac had given me all the time, and could switch it out for other pieces when the mood struck me.

"Yes, I do," I said.

The shop owner must have noted the way we were lingering at that one case, because she hurried over and said, "Would you like to see it?"

I told her I would, and she extracted the necklace from the case and handed it over to me. It was heavy against the palm of my hand, almost as heavy as the amulet I currently wore. And although I'd never been the type to be much into crystals and stones and all their supposed properties and powers, I couldn't quite ignore the way a tingle ran up my hand as soon as the necklace rested against my palm.

Was it magic, like the compass I'd found a few weeks ago?

But no, this wasn't exactly that kind of sensa-

tion. Maybe it was nothing more than the energy
of the turquoise stone, a really gorgeous piece in a
soft robin's egg blue with intricate veining in dark
brown or maybe even black. Although I definitely
couldn't call myself an expert, I'd begun to learn
the differences between the various types of
turquoise, the bright bold blue of Sleeping Beauty,
the pale, pale sky color of Dry Creek. And while I
didn't know which mine this particular piece had
come from, I knew that anything with this sort of
veining was very desirable.

A mirror sat on the counter, and so I held the
necklace up to my throat, almost obscuring the
amulet. It was enough to show me how it would
look when I wore it—eye-catching, unusual. I'd
never been the type to collect jewelry, was definitely
lacking the magpie gene, and yet I was almost startled by how badly I wanted it.

A tremor of warning went through me. Was
this a honey pot, like the picture frame I'd brought
home from a local store last month, only to
discover it was a lure set out by a demon so he
could track down where I'd been living?

Almost as soon as that thought passed through
my mind, I set it aside. I didn't know exactly what
was going on with this pendant, but it didn't feel
the way that honey pot had. The enchanted picture
frame hadn't given me any signal that it was magical, had only made me want to take it home,

whereas I'd definitely felt something as soon as I lifted the raven-cradled piece of turquoise in my hand.

There was something else going on here, even if I didn't yet know what it was.

"I love it," I said, and my father smiled.

"Then we'll take it," he told the clerk, an older woman with gray-streaked black hair. She looked more Hispanic than Native American, although I'd already learned that the bloodlines here were so mixed, it was often difficult to tell the difference.

"Would you like to wear it?" she asked.

Because Isaac had told me I needed to wear the protection amulet whenever I was out in public, I knew replacing it with my new pendant probably wasn't a very good idea. "No, you can put it in a box for now," I said.

Maybe my father looked ever so slightly disappointed, but he still smiled at the clerk as he handed over his black Amex card. "Thank you," he told her.

She went ahead and rang up the sale while I did my best to not look at the total when she gave my father the receipt to sign. Even from a sideways angle, I could still tell the piece was three figures, but I figured the damage could have been a lot worse.

We walked out of the shop and headed back toward my place, since by that point it was getting past five o'clock. "I hope all this wandering didn't keep you from your dinner prep," my father commented as we turned down my street.

"Nope," I said cheerfully. "It's all in the crockpot—all I have to do is heat up some rolls and throw together a salad."

He looked relieved by my reply. "Sounds great."

I was sure it did. While my mother didn't make him follow a strict keto diet the way she did, I had a feeling it had been a long time since a basket of rolls had graced their dining room table.

As for me, I'd been blessed with a great metabolism, so as long as I didn't overdo it, I could eat pretty much whatever I wanted. Also, since coming to Santa Fe—and being lucky enough to have landed in a house located close to downtown —I found myself walking a lot of the time, a good way to replace the activity from a job that had kept me on my feet for most of the day.

The house was quiet as we entered, reassuring me that no supernatural mischief had taken place while we were out. My father excused himself to go use the bathroom, and I pulled my phone out of my purse to make sure I hadn't missed any texts or calls. All quiet, which meant Isaac should be over at six-thirty as planned.

I went ahead and started to set the table. When my father came back out to the dining room, he asked if he could help. Of course I told him I had things handled, and then I suggested that maybe he could catch up on any business while I was getting things ready.

"In fact, you can go in the office if you need a little privacy," I told him. "It's the room at the end of the hall."

He looked a little apologetic...but he also didn't turn down my offer. "I should probably check on a few things," he admitted. "It shouldn't take long."

"Take as long as you need," I said. "Isaac won't be here for another forty-five minutes or so."

A quick thank-you, and then my father headed down the hallway and went into the office. After he was gone, I returned to setting the table, and then paused and pulled the box with the raven pendant out of my purse, which I'd set down on the peninsula in the kitchen.

Surely it would be okay to wear the pendant here, where I was safely guarded by all the wards on the house, not to mention the protection candle that still burned steadily on the granite kitchen counter. As usual, I was wearing black, and I thought the turquoise stone would stand out that much more against such a neutral backdrop.

That seemed to decide things. I reached up and undid the clasp of the amulet, feeling a little strange as I did so; I hadn't removed it since the day Isaac hung the piece around my neck several weeks earlier. However, because hordes of demons didn't descend the second I pulled it away from my neck, I thought I was probably safe in taking it off, if only temporarily.

I placed the amulet inside one of the inner pockets of my purse, figuring I'd put it back on at the end of the evening. Then I undid the clasp of the raven necklace and hung it around my throat.

Immediately, the dining room disappeared. Instead, I saw a small, somewhat shabby store, with a case of jewelry in front of me and shelves crowded with audio equipment, cameras, and even guns lining the wall behind the counter.

As far as I could tell, the place looked like the world's most stereotypical pawn shop.

And there was the red-haired woman I believed was my mother, reaching up to undo the necklace she wore before handing it across the counter to the man who stood there. He looked Hispanic, probably in his late fifties or early sixties, with thinning gray-streaked hair and a deeply lined face. After taking the necklace from my mother, he turned the piece over in his hands, then went to weigh it on the small scale he had placed next to the cash register.

Some haggling took place afterward, although, since watching this vision was like viewing security camera footage, there was no sound, only the moving images of the red-haired woman and the owner of the shop, and so I couldn't hear what they were saying. However, the content of their discussion appeared obvious enough, because a minute later, the man opened the cash register and counted out a batch of twenties and laid them on the countertop.

The red-haired woman hesitated for just a second or two, as though she'd been hoping she might get more for the piece. But then she scooped up the bills and shoved them in her purse, not even bothering to pick up the pawn ticket the man tried to give her. Clearly, she had no intention of returning to redeem the piece she'd just hocked.

The necklace that now lay against my throat, heavy and cool. And once again I had to wonder whether I was truly a lodestone, or whether I was only being attracted to items she had left behind for me to find, like a trail of magically charged breadcrumbs.

I didn't know. And even though I was burning to ask Isaac about the necklace and what it might mean, I knew such a discussion would have to wait until we were alone. No way in the world could I bring up that kind of subject around my father. No, we'd have a friendly, perfectly normal dinner conversation, and then, once he'd headed back to his luxury B&B, Isaac and I would have a chat.

Almost as though my thoughts had summoned him, the doorbell rang then. I grabbed my purse and shoved it into one of the storage cupboards under the kitchen peninsula, since there wasn't time to take it back to the bedroom the way I'd planned, and then hurried over to the door and opened it.

Isaac waited outside, crutches propped under his arms. Even though he'd been able to stand on his own for longer and longer periods, he still needed those crutches by the end of the day.

A quick kiss of greeting as I let him in. Once he straightened, his gaze went right to the raven and turquoise necklace I wore, and questions filled his eyes. However, he didn't have a chance to say anything before my father entered the living room.

"Dad," I said, glad I sounded completely normal, unruffled and casual, "this is Isaac. Isaac, this is my father, Gerald Briggs."

The two men shook hands, with my father directing just the quickest of glances toward Isaac's crutches—which hadn't interfered with the hand-shake at all, since Isaac was used to negotiating those sorts of social interactions. Of course, my father was too well-mannered to comment, but I could tell he was just the slightest bit curious, as I'd never mentioned anything about Isaac's accident or the years of convalescence that had followed.

"It's very nice to meet you, Mr. Briggs," Isaac said, to which my father immediately shook his head.

"Gerald, please," he replied. "No need to stand on ceremony." He sent a quick glance over at me. "Penny, is there anything you need us to help you with?"

"Nothing at all," I said at once. "Well, except to maybe open the wine while I bring in the stuff from the kitchen."

"I think we can manage that," he said, and the two men headed toward the dining room while I made a beeline for the kitchen.

Soon enough, everything was laid out on the dining room table, and my father poured some cabernet for each of us. Isaac raised his glass at once and said, "Welcome to Santa Fe."

We clinked our goblets and drank, and my father said, "It's a beautiful town. I can see why Penny would want to settle down here."

Some men might have blinked at the phrase "settle down," but Isaac only responded, "You've never been here before?"

"Unfortunately, no," my father said. "Santa Fe has always been kind of on my bucket list, but I'd never managed to make it here until now."

Meaning, I guessed, that my mother had absolutely no desire to visit New Mexico, not when she could be jetting off to New York or Paris or Dubai instead, which meant my father had never managed to squeeze in a trip to Santa Fe. Probably the only reason he'd managed this little jaunt at all was that he'd only be gone for a couple of days, not long enough for my mother to get too annoyed by his absence.

"Well," Isaac said, "I hope you'll have plenty of time to do more exploring."

My father sent a quick glance at me before saying with a smile, "I'm afraid not. I could only fit a couple of days away into my schedule, so I need to head back tomorrow."

"But we got to visit some museums and galleries and shops today," I put in, "so at least Dad was able to get a taste of what Santa Fe has to offer. And maybe next time it'll be for a longer trip."

"I certainly hope so," he said.

From there, we chatted about all the other things to see and do around town, including Santa Fe's world-famous opera. My mother was a fiend about the opera—mostly because it gave her a reason to get really dressed up—and we speculated whether the lure of the Santa Fe Opera might be enough to get her to visit as well. Not that I had any great desire to see her any time soon, but I knew my best chance of having my father make a return trip would be to bring her along as well.

He agreed that might be feasible, and then he said, "So, Isaac. Penny tells me you own a business here in Santa Fe?"

Isaac nodded. Now his expression appeared faintly amused, as though he'd guessed my father was trying to find out whether the man I'd been dating was worthy of his daughter. So far, the two of them seemed to get along great—I could already tell my dad thought Isaac was a much higher caliber of person than my ex had been—but he still probably wanted to know that I hadn't hooked up with a deadbeat.

"Yes, it's called The Enchanted Circle," Isaac replied. "It's downtown, about a ten-minute walk from here. The place was actually my mother's store—I inherited it about seven years ago."

"What kind of store?" my father asked, then took a bite of pot roast.

Here we go, I thought, but I knew I needed to keep silent.

"Kind of a New Age shop," Isaac said, imperturbable as always. "Books and crystals, mostly. Some jewelry, and things like Tarot and oracle cards. The usual."

Through all this, my father hadn't even blinked. Then he said, "Is there a lot of interest in that sort of thing here in Santa Fe?"

"Absolutely. Santa Fe is a very spiritual town. Our roots go deep here."

A brief silence as my father absorbed that comment. Then he nodded very slightly to himself, as though acknowledging that, whatever he might think of New Age woo-woo, no one would be able to keep a shop running for all those years on an expensive piece of real estate like downtown Santa Fe unless they were very good at what they did.

"I got that impression," he said after that little pause. "Maybe that's what you liked about the place, Penny. There's a real sense of history here."

"Exactly," I replied. "I know Southern California has its attractions, but no one can really accuse it of being a hotbed of history."

My remark lightened the mood a bit, as I'd hoped it would, and he chuckled. "No, that's for sure. And maybe some history was exactly what was missing for you."

Well, that and finding a man who seemed to accept me for exactly who I was, crazy magical talents and unknown bio-mom and the whole shebang. I'd always told myself I didn't need a man to make my life complete—or at least, that had been my mantra after Dave and I split up—but having Isaac at my side had definitely made the madness of the past month a lot easier to handle.

"I think you're right," I said. "And maybe it is partly biology, since it seems as though my bio-mom might have come from around here."

My father's clear blue eyes sharpened a little. "What makes you say that?"

Heat colored my cheeks a bit. Where had those words even come from? True, my biological mother's eggs had been donated at a clinic in Albuquerque, but I guessed it was finding the necklace in Santa Fe that made me think she must have pawned it somewhere in New Mexico. Maybe not here in Santa Fe itself, since even I knew that pawned jewelry could really make the rounds once its owners had forfeited it, but still.

"Just a feeling, I guess," I said, knowing I sounded sheepish. "And that my egg came from Albuquerque."

"Did you feel this way when you were living down there?" Isaac asked. His expression didn't show anything beyond simple curiosity, although I thought he'd already guessed there was more going on here than met the eye.

"No," I replied at once, since that was only the truth. "There's definitely something special about Santa Fe that I didn't feel in Albuquerque. But this could just be me being all woo-woo and nothing else."

Both my father and Isaac chuckled at that comment, as I'd hoped they would. After that, my father asked Isaac some questions about Santa Fe real estate, giving me the impression that he wouldn't be averse to buying property here if he could get my mother to agree. Isaac responded with more expertise than I would have guessed, reminding me that one of his sisters-in-law was a real estate agent here in town, and so he probably stayed more up to date on that sort of thing than most people.

The meal began to wind down, and at length my father balled up his napkin and placed it on the table. "This has been wonderful, Penny," he said, "but I have a car picking me up at eight-thirty tomorrow so I can get an early flight back to L.A., so I think I should probably turn in."

Even though I'd known he was heading to Southern California the next morning, for some reason, I hadn't thought it would be so early, had hoped that maybe we could meet for breakfast before he left. "That early?"

He didn't quite grimace. "Yes—I have a meeting in Brentwood at one that I couldn't cancel, so I need to get moving early."

Since there obviously wasn't any point in arguing, I just nodded and stood as my father rose from the table and Isaac got his crutches, which he'd propped against the kitchen peninsula, and stood up as well. "It was very nice to meet you, Gerald," he said.

"And I'm glad I had the chance to meet you, Isaac," my father responded. "It looks like you're taking good care of my daughter."

I couldn't help wincing at that remark, but Isaac only smiled and said, "When she lets me."

After that, we walked my father to the door, and I gave him a quick, fierce hug. Getting to see him had meant a lot more to me than I'd thought it would, possibly because he'd offered a bit of permanence in what currently felt like a constantly shifting existence. "Have a safe flight, Dad," I said. "Can you text me when you land in L.A., just so I know everything went okay?"

"Absolutely," he said. "Good night, you two."

And he headed down the steps, striding briskly once he got to the front path. Because the B&B where he was staying was only a few blocks away, he hadn't even bothered to call an Uber or a Lyft, but would walk back to his hotel. This part of Santa Fe was safe enough, and I knew I didn't need to worry about him—or rather, I wouldn't have worried if I didn't know that other things lurked in the darkness besides muggers.

I lingered on the front porch until he was out of sight, and then I closed the door. Isaac stood a few feet away, still propped up on his crutches, his gaze now almost speculative.

Then he said, "Do you want to tell me about that necklace?"

Chapter 4
The Turquoise Trail

My fingers went up to touch one of the sterling ravens, the metal cool against my fingertips. "My father bought it for me at a shop downtown," I said. "I was immediately drawn to it."

Now Isaac's dark eyes sparked with interest. "You were?"

I nodded, then went over to him and said, "Let's go sit down in the living room."

His gaze strayed toward the dining room table, where the detritus of our meal still waited. However, he didn't suggest we should clean up first, but only replied, "All right."

We went and sat down on one of the couches. Because it was a cold night, I'd gotten a fire going in the hearth, and the room felt warm and cozy...and the sort of place that was very far away from enchanted necklaces and curses and demons.

However, since this space had been invaded by a demon not once, but twice, I knew it wasn't as safe as it looked.

All the same, it was comforting to have Isaac sitting there next to me, to have him wait while I gathered my thoughts. "I think this necklace belonged to my mother," I said.

His eyebrows lifted slightly. "What makes you think that?"

So I explained how I'd felt drawn to the necklace out of all the others in that case—and all the others I'd seen during my father's and my wanderings around downtown and its various shops and galleries—and how, when I'd put it on this evening, I'd witnessed that scene of my biological mother handing the necklace over in exchange for a wad of twenty-dollar bills.

"She seemed like she was in a hurry," I said.

"Frightened?" Isaac asked.

I paused as I did my best to re-create the scene in my mind, the way she'd been waiting at the counter, how she hadn't bothered to get the pawn ticket from the shop's owner, as if she'd known she'd never be back to reclaim her property. Now I could see that she'd been dressed normally enough, in jeans and an embroidered peasant-style top, with sandals on her feet. Her long hair had been pulled back into a loose ponytail, showing silver hoops in her ears.

"Not exactly," I said slowly, picking through the details of the scene in my mind. "Just...urgent. Like she knew she needed to get out of there as quickly as possible."

Isaac's brows drew together as he considered that bit of information. "As though someone was on her trail?"

"Maybe," I said. "It's hard to say for sure, because I could only see what was happening, not hear what they were saying. If I'd been able to hear her voice, it might have been easier to tell if she sounded frightened. Mostly, though, she just looked like someone who was trying to get some business handled so she could go on to her next destination."

"Wherever that was."

I lifted my shoulders in a helpless shrug. Had she sold the necklace before or after she'd gone to the fertility clinic in Albuquerque to sell her eggs? Before, I guessed. I still didn't know where she'd died, why she'd been fleeing in terror through the red rock canyon that would become her tomb, but I knew it probably hadn't been anywhere around Santa Fe or Albuquerque, since red rock formations weren't super common in this part of the state.

"There's still so much we don't know," I said.

"But this gave me another piece of information... and my father provided some more."

Briefly, I related what my father had told me about my biological half-brother, how the other three eggs had been disposed of when the clinic in Los Angeles was closed.

Isaac seemed almost alarmed by this news. Eyes narrowing, he asked, "This half-brother of yours died the same way your ex-husband did?"

Once again, an uncomfortable little chill worked its way down my back. "Apparently," I said. "A heart attack in his sleep, even though he was healthy and only twenty-nine. But the police couldn't find any evidence of foul play, and so they had to rule it a death from natural causes."

A long silence as Isaac's hands clenched on the knees of his pants, and his expression turned very grim. "It's easy to make a death via magic look as though it was natural," he said. "But I'm worried there was nothing natural about it. This was in Colorado?"

"Yes," I said, now feeling colder than ever, even though the fire blazing a few feet away had warmed the room to a comfortable level. "Denver, was what my father said."

Once again, Isaac went quiet, his elegant jaw tense as he seemed to turn over one theory after another, each of them more chilling than the next. "Penny, what if your biological grandmother discovered this half-brother's existence and had him killed?"

I hunched my shoulders, not sure I wanted to acknowledge that Isaac's suggestion might be possible...or even plausible. "But why would she do that?" I asked. "That one demon told me she was coming after me because she wanted to make sure she had her witchy granddaughter back in the family. Why would she kill someone who would have inherited the family powers?"

"Because he probably *didn't* inherit those powers," Isaac said. His voice was now calm, but it held an edge I didn't like very much, the tone of a man who was being forced to acknowledge an unpleasant truth. "Like I told you before, the chances of a male child inheriting a witch family's gifts are very low. What if your biological grandmother somehow discovered the existence of her grandson, but also discovered that he didn't have any magic at all? If she was ruthless enough to have her own daughter killed, I don't see why she wouldn't dispose of someone she saw as lesser, especially when his very existence proved her daughter's defiance."

None of this sounded good at all to me...but at the same time, I had to admit I could see that scenario playing out in real life, especially since we knew the woman had basically put a demonic hit out on her daughter. Maybe the demon had been lying, but I didn't think so. In this particular case, the truth had hurt far more than any lie would have.

Right then, I was very, very glad that Dr. Lightman's clinic in Los Angeles had never gotten around to implanting those other three eggs. If they had—and if those children had grown to adulthood—then it was entirely possible my bio-grandmother would have been gunning for them as well.

In my case, at least I didn't have to worry about her trying to kill me, only doing her best to have me dragged back to wherever she was lurking so I could become part of her unholy coven.

If she even had a coven. To tell the truth, I still didn't know all that much about how most witches operated. Isaac was very much a solo practitioner, even if his mother had trained him. For all I knew, my grandmother was working entirely on her own, which could only be a good thing. No matter how powerful she was, going up against one witch had to be a lot easier than taking on a whole coven.

True, she apparently had a nasty habit of sending demons to do her dirty work, but since all had been quiet on the Santa Fe front lately, she must have realized that particular tactic wasn't working so well for her. Because demons weren't the most loyal servants, it didn't appear as though they'd told her where I was living, or no doubt she would have appeared on my doorstep by now.

"I suppose I don't want to believe it's possible that she killed someone just because he didn't meet her standards," I said, then continued before Isaac could comment. "On the other hand, she's certainly shown she doesn't have much in the way of scruples, so I guess I can see how she might have done something so terrible."

As I spoke, I found myself wishing we hadn't finished our bottle of cabernet with dinner. This new wrinkle made me think I could use another drink. However, opening a second bottle didn't seem like a very good idea, so I told myself I'd just have to muddle through. At least I still had a faint wine buzz from the glass and a half I'd drunk with the pot roast I'd made.

For a moment, Isaac was silent, although his somber expression didn't change, making me think his thoughts were far from pleasant. When he spoke, however, he sounded brisk enough, as if he'd decided it was better to put aside our speculations about my bio-grandmother's motives and focus on something a little closer to home.

"Have you had any other visions since putting on the necklace?"

"No," I replied at once, since at least that was a question I could answer with some conviction. "As soon as you rang the doorbell, that glimpse I had of the pawn shop went away."

He didn't seem too surprised by this—visions were fragile things, and any intrusion by the outside world could make them blow away like fog under a strong wind. "You should try sleeping with it under your pillow," he suggested.

That same stratagem had worked with the eyeglasses I'd found in an antique mall in Albuquerque, glasses that had given me my first glimpse of the woman who was my biological mother. At the same time, the vision I'd seen was terrible, a cinematic view of the place that had become her grave, and I didn't know whether I really wanted to see what the necklace might show me as I slept. The vision of the pawn shop had been benign enough...but the next one might not be.

But I didn't argue. The necklace was the only real lead we had right now when it came to learning more about my bio-mom's identity, and so I knew it would be stupid to avoid using it just because I was worried about seeing something equally as gruesome as that vultures' feast.

One hand went up to touch the necklace at my throat. "Okay," I said. "I can't promise anything, but—"

Isaac leaned over and kissed me gently on the mouth, effectively cutting off my words. "I don't expect you to make that kind of promise," he said after we both came up for air. "And I know what you see might be...difficult. But we don't have a lot of other options."

No, we didn't. The necklace was the one thing I had that seemed even more connected to the woman who'd given me her red hair than the eyeglasses I'd found a month earlier, and I'd be stupid to ignore it just because I was getting the heebie-jeebies.

"If I see anything, I'll let you know."

He bent and kissed me again, but a gentle brush of his lips against my cheek, not the passionate, cabernet-tasting kiss we'd shared a moment earlier. Right then, the ache of needing him was so strong, it was practically a physical cramp. I did my best to ignore it, however, because whenever Isaac and I might end up consummating our relationship, it wouldn't be tonight.

In a much different tone, he said, "Your father seems like a nice man."

A little relieved by the change of subject, I returned, "Well, he can be."

That response made Isaac lift an eyebrow, so I figured I'd better elaborate.

"I mean, he's never been anything but a good father to me," I went on. "But some of the people he's had business dealings with might have a difference of opinion over that whole 'nice' thing."

"Ruthless?" Isaac asked, although he still seemed amused rather than put off.

"When necessary," I said. "I don't think he's ever done anything technically illegal, but you don't turn fifty thousand dollars in seed money from your parents into a half-billion-dollar fortune without stepping on a few toes."

My careless mention of such a sum made Isaac's eyes widen slightly. Oh, he knew my family had money, but it wasn't until this moment that I'd baldly stated exactly how much money we were talking about.

"Yes, I suppose I can see that," he managed after a moment.

"Anyway," I said, glad he'd been apparently willing to let the matter go. Not that I would ever believe such a thing of him, but it was still good to know he didn't care about my family's wealth. "He obviously approves of you, and that's the important thing. He was never a huge fan of Dave. I'd say that made him a good judge of character, but since he seems to be pretty blind when it comes to my mother, I'll withhold judgment."

"I'm sorry she's made things so difficult for you."

There was nothing but sympathy and compassion in those deep, dark eyes. While Dave had called my mother the b-word on more than one occasion, there had never been any follow-up as to how having a woman like her as my mother must have made my life a living hell. No, he'd always just assumed that because we had lots of money, I really couldn't have wanted for anything. One time I'd tried to tell him there were different ways of being poor besides a lack of cash, but the argument had flown right over his head, and I'd given up after that.

I reached over and took Isaac's hand, squeezing it gently. No point in telling him I was over it, not when I really wasn't. No, I just said, "She's mostly out of my life now. What's really important to me is learning as much as I can about my biological mother."

His fingers closed on mine. Voice low but intense, he replied, "I know. And I'll do everything I can to help you every step of the way."

———

Because it was a weeknight and the hour was already edging past ten o'clock, Isaac didn't stay too much longer after that, although he insisted on helping me clear the table and load the dishwasher. I knew offering what assistance he could was important to him, and so I didn't bother to argue. After we were done, I walked him to the door, and he gave me a lingering goodnight kiss.

"Call if you need to," he said. "I don't care what time it is."

Had any other man ever given me such an open-ended invitation?

All the same, I wouldn't abuse the privilege. "I will if it's anything earth-shattering," I told him. "But otherwise, I'll give you a call around noon."

He told me that sounded good, and then headed down the front walk to his van. Not for the first time, I wondered how much longer he would continue driving the specially equipped vehicle, since I hadn't seen him use his wheelchair for almost two weeks now.

Well, that decision was between him and his doctor, or maybe him and his physical therapist. I knew he must have a lot of money invested in the van, and even though his progress had been amazing lately, it was never a good thing to count your chickens before they hatched.

I went ahead and got ready for bed, and unclasped the raven necklace from around my throat and tucked it under the pillow, taking care to make sure it lay completely flat and that the chain wasn't kinked or twisted in some way that might need unraveling the next morning, or that it was in an awkward position that might damage the setting if I got too restless during the night. Even as I carefully put it in place, I found myself wondering whether this was such a good idea.

Maybe I wouldn't see anything at all—the first vision had only appeared after I fastened the piece around my throat, and so maybe it needed physical contact with me to open that strange conduit between the past and the present, the one that some strange gift hidden in my gray matter was able to interpret and transform into images as clear as though I was watching them on my high-def TV. True, putting them under my pillow had worked with the eyeglasses, but maybe the enchantment on the necklace had taken a slightly different form.

But I wouldn't know for sure unless I tried, and so I realized I was committed to this course of action...no matter what happened.

After I turned on the white noise machine on my bedside and shut off the lamp, I lay down and stared at the ceiling. Behind the sound of rain coming from the gadget on the nightstand, I could hear the hum of the furnace in the background, sending warm air through the vents, since it was supposed to get close to freezing overnight.

Even though I was tired—it had been a long and active day, what with wandering around downtown Santa Fe with my father—I still felt restless, unable to find a comfortable position, despite the way I generally could fall asleep within five minutes or so of my head hitting the pillow. And I couldn't even blame my restiveness on the necklace beneath that same pillow, because I honestly couldn't sense its presence there at all.

No, I had a feeling I didn't want to fall asleep because I didn't want to see whatever visions the necklace might choose to send me.

Which sort of negated the purpose of this whole exercise. I blew out a breath and shifted onto my side, telling myself I needed to sleep, that there was every chance I wouldn't see anything at all. If that turned out to be the case, then I'd try putting on the necklace again in the morning. Either way, I knew I needed to let myself be open to my mother's past, as it very well could affect my future.

And eventually, I did fall asleep. My dreams were a jumble of my day—I had a vision of my father and I munching on tacos as we strolled the halls of the Georgia O'Keeffe Museum, an activity that would never be allowed in real life, since all food and drink were strictly forbidden in those hallowed halls. There was also something about being on a panel at a convention I thought was probably supposed to be Comic Con, since all the celebrities flanking me were from various Marvel movies. It was definitely one of those embarrassment dreams where you know you're not supposed to be there but can't figure out how to gracefully escape without anyone noticing.

That dream faded, though, and the next thing I saw was definitely I-25 southbound heading toward Albuquerque, since I recognized the highway sign that told me Cochiti Lake was the next exit, and New Mexico's largest population center still some thirty miles away. Once again, I saw the redheaded woman I somehow knew was my biological mother, this time sitting behind the wheel of some big dinosaur of a car that looked to be '70s vintage, an ugly metallic green with a black vinyl top that was peeling in places. She had the windows down, her long coppery hair blowing in the breeze, and she was tapping her fingers on the steering wheel as she apparently sang along with the radio. Like my other vision from the necklace, there wasn't any sound, and so I couldn't hear the song, nor tell whether her voice was pretty or woefully out of tune.

However, she definitely looked like someone who didn't have a care in the world, or who was on the run from a murderous parent who used demons as her thugs. And though I knew people had a tendency to hide what was going on in their hearts and in their heads, you'd think when she was alone like this, she would have let the façade slip, would have revealed something of what had sent her on the run in the first place.

The vision faded after that, and I moved into a dreamless sleep and stayed there until a ray of light pushing past the blinds woke me a little after seven-thirty. I blinked, then sat up, doing my best to catch hold of the vision before it began to fade from my memory.

In fact, I got out of bed and hurried into the office to retrieve one of my sketchpads. Pencil in hand, I hurried back into bed so I could pull the covers up around me and enjoy some of their lingering warmth, then began quickly sketching the outlines of the scene—the big green car on the highway...the sign at the side of the road...the woman with her long hair caught by the breeze.

When I was done, I thought I'd gotten down a fairly accurate rendering of the vision. No obvious branding on the car, but it still looked distinctive enough that I hoped I might be able to figure out what it was by poking around on the internet and studying various '70s-vintage sedans to see if any of them looked like the vehicle my bio-mom had been driving.

Whether that would help me at all, I had no idea. Just because I was able to determine that the car had been a Buick or a Pontiac or whatever wouldn't necessarily get me any closer to learning where she'd died, or precisely why.

But it was something. At the moment, I'd have to go with it and hope for the best.

Chapter 5
Car Buff

My first searches, performed while I drank my morning cup of coffee and had some sourdough toast, didn't seem terribly conclusive. Or rather, it seemed there were a lot more metallic green cars with black vinyl tops driving around in the 1970s than I'd thought.

However, when I returned to my laptop after showering and getting dressed, I had a bit more luck. It turned out the 1973 Buick LeSabre had been offered with a black vinyl top and a metallic paint called Willow Green, and its outlines pretty perfectly matched the car my mother had been driving.

Why she'd been driving a twenty-year-old car, I didn't know. Was it something she'd bought cheap while on the run, or had she stolen it from her witch—in both senses of the term—mother?

As usual, it seemed as though the more facts I dug up, the more questions floated to the surface at the same time.

And while the identification of the vintage car from my vision was an interesting factoid, I didn't think it merited calling Isaac first thing in the morning...or my version of first thing, anyway, since by that point it was nearly ten o'clock. I'd go ahead and call once I knew Isaac was safely at work rather than wait until noon, although I didn't know whether he'd have too many insights to offer.

Because it was probably quiet at the store that Wednesday morning, he picked up after the first ring. "Penny?" he said. "How was your sleep?"

That he'd asked the question in such an oblique way told me he actually did have at least one customer in the store, even though he'd answered the phone pretty quickly. "Fine," I told him. "I saw something, but I don't know whether it was really that important. Can you take a break at lunch?"

"Sure," he said, a reply that made me relax a bit. If he was really slammed at work, he often had to discreetly eat a sandwich while continuing to help customers, but if he thought he'd be able to steal away for a real sit-down lunch somewhere, then he probably wasn't too busy today. "Meet me at Tia Maria's at noon?"

"See you then," I promised him, and then hung

up so he could get back to his patrons. Twelve o'clock wasn't that far off; I'd work on storyboards during the intervening time and head over to the restaurant a little before noon. It was a popular place, and so I knew I wanted to give myself some extra time in order to get a decent seat.

As planned, I put down my pencil and picked up my purse at about a quarter to twelve—and put a hand to my neck to reassure myself the protection amulet still hung there—and started walking over to the restaurant. I hadn't gotten more than a block before my phone pinged. At once, I pulled it out of my purse, worried that Isaac might have needed to cancel our lunch date for some reason.

But no, the message was from my father.

Just landed in L.A., it said. *Heading over to Brentwood now. Thanks again for dinner last night. Give Isaac my best.*

Short and to the point, but seeing the text still made me happy. My father had gotten back to Southern California safely, and he'd even included a mention of Isaac in his message. Some people might not have seen that as a big deal, but I knew better. If he hadn't liked Isaac, my father wouldn't have mentioned him at all. As it was, I could tell he approved of the current man in my life.

In contrast to my cheerful mood, the weather that day was cloudy and downright gloomy, even though there hadn't been any rain yet, just a cold wind that made me glad I'd bought my pretty teal wool coat down in Albuquerque while I was still living there and that it was warm enough to keep out even the sharpest gusts. Maybe it was the threatening skies outside or just the simple fact of it being a quiet Wednesday in November, but either way, I was able to get a nice booth at the window, where I told the hostess I was waiting for someone and would wait to order until he arrived.

She smiled at me and said that was no problem, and so I settled against the seat back and watched the people come and go on San Francisco Street, a lot of them obviously tourists, since they tended to travel in packs, rather than the solo walkers who were probably on their way to lunch or running some other errand during their noon break.

About five minutes after I'd sat down, Isaac came in. He was using his crutches but didn't look particularly fatigued by his walk over here, telling me he was having a good day despite being out late at my place the night before.

He bent and placed a kiss on my cheek before taking a seat on the other side of the booth, and I found myself flushing a little, even as I realized how glad I was that he was okay with such a public display of affection. There might not have been anything remotely formal about our relationship, and yet I doubted he would have kissed me in a restaurant he'd been going to since he was a little kid if he didn't mind signaling to all of Santa Fe that he was dating a red-haired newcomer to town.

"Am I late?" he asked as he settled his napkin on his lap.

"Not at all," I replied. "I just thought I'd come a little early to make sure we got a decent place to sit."

A nod, and then he waited as the hostess came over and asked what we'd like to drink. I requested hot tea, since I still felt a bit chilly from the walk over, while Isaac ordered the iced version of the same beverage. With that business handled, he sent me an inquiring glance.

"I did see something," I told him, and he gave a very small nod, as though my words confirmed what he'd already been thinking. "I'm just not sure how important it was."

I didn't have a chance to go further than that, however, because the waitress showed up then and inquired about our food orders. Because Isaac knew the menu by heart, he went ahead and ordered first, giving me a chance to take a quick glance at the offerings and make my decision. With that business handled—and after the hostess returned with our drinks—I felt it was safe to go on with my story.

So, I told Isaac about what I'd seen, and how I'd been able to determine that my mother had been driving on I-25 southbound in a 1973 Buick LeSabre with a Willow Green paint job.

"I'm just not sure what any of it is supposed to mean, though," I concluded, knowing my tone sounded a little too plaintive.

"Well, if nothing else, it shows your biological mother left Santa Fe of her own free will," Isaac said, then took a sip of his iced tea. "There wasn't anyone in the car with her, right?"

"Right," I replied. The vision hadn't showed me a whole lot, but it had definitely made it clear that my bio-mom had been alone in her big gas-guzzler. A memory of my chilly walk over to the restaurant prompted me to add, "And I'm guessing it must have been sometime in the summer, or I doubt she would have been driving with her windows open like that."

"Which makes sense," Isaac said. "Because your vision of the canyon had to be sometime during monsoon season, based on the way you described the skies."

I'd almost forgotten about that particular detail, but he was right. Since I'd moved to New Mexico at the tail end of September, I hadn't gotten a chance to experience those monsoon storms for myself, but the timelines did seem to match up. Where had she been headed in her Buick as she sang along to the radio? Judging by how carefree she'd looked in my vision, I doubted she had any idea she had a date with destiny in some unknown red rock canyon where her body would lie undiscovered for years and years.

"I wish the vision had shown me a different stretch of highway, though," I told him. "She couldn't have been too far from Santa Fe during that flash, which doesn't tell me a whole heck of a lot about where she might have been headed. From there, she could have continued south, deeper into New Mexico, or she could have gone east on I-40 toward Texas or west into Arizona."

"West seems more likely, considering the red rocks in your first visions of her," Isaac said, his tone now thoughtful. He didn't seem particularly disturbed by what I'd just related, but then, why would he be? This vision had had a very different feel to it, had let me see a little more of my bio-mom's personality. She'd looked friendly and cheerful, and like someone I might have been friends with.

No way in the world could I imagine the woman who'd raised me singing along to the radio in such a carefree way.

"So...Arizona?" I asked.

"Maybe. I'm not sure, though, since everything else you've seen of this woman seems to have been centered here in New Mexico."

Including the artifacts she'd left behind for me to discover. Had she been on her way to hide something else as she drove along in her green Buick? If so, what had it been?

Those patriarch's tears, whatever those were supposed to be?

While I thought I could understand her reasons for being so oblique with her clues—she'd obviously wanted to make sure that if the riddle fell into the wrong hands, it couldn't be deciphered too easily—it didn't make me feel any better about our absolute lack of progress in being able to puzzle out the words' true meaning.

"I think you're right," I said, even though I couldn't have told Isaac with any certainty precisely why I thought his theory was a true one.

Our waitress showed up with the food right then, and so we had to abandon our discussion for a few minutes as we dug into our meals. Once we were both a little more fortified, however, Isaac spoke again.

"So, we should keep our focus here in New Mexico for now. Where exactly this is all going to lead, I don't know, but I'm certain we'll find the answers not too far from home."

I wished I had his confidence. At the same time, though, I had to admit we hadn't gathered any clues that seemed to be pointing outside the state. If nothing else, staying focused here would make our task a little easier. New Mexico was big enough on its own—no point in making this particular job any harder than it already was.

After taking another bite of my chicken enchilada, I said, "I wish I knew why she looked so cheerful in my vision. She definitely didn't look like someone on the run from supernatural bad guys."

Isaac had broken off a piece of sopapilla—a fluffy little pillow of dough that was often served with New Mexican meals—and was carefully spreading some butter and honey on it. After he was done with his bite, he replied, "It's possible that she'd just gotten done hiding the sword and the riddle in the mountains outside Cimarron. If that's what was really going on, I suppose you could see why she'd be feeling pretty pleased with herself. It was a complicated piece of magic, not one that many witches would even dare to attempt."

He had a point there. Because I was such a fledgling witch, I didn't have the foggiest idea as to how you'd go about creating a hidden chamber inside a mountain, let alone enchanting it so it would only open to the person who held the key she'd cached in that rock formation north of Taos. I could see how managing such a feat might make a person feel invincible.

But not so invincible that she could live without money, which would explain why she'd stopped in

Santa Fe to pawn her necklace and bring in a couple hundred bucks to help her continue on her journey. Back in the early '90s, that few hundred dollars would have gotten her a lot farther than it would today. Had she been planning to leave the state altogether after she donated her eggs in Albuquerque? Because it seemed as though she'd only donated a few, I had to believe she'd gone through the process just once, figuring she would make enough money from the procedure to get her wherever she planned to go. However, she would've still needed some cash to live on in the interim, as the brief research I'd done on the subject had told me the egg-donation process could take as long as a month.

"I wouldn't even know where to start doing that kind of thing," I remarked, and Isaac smiled.

"Neither would I," he admitted. "But obviously, she was able to accomplish the job, and obviously, you were strong enough to find the things she left for you to discover. That means she must have intended for you to locate whatever she was referring to in the riddle."

"Well, I hope she wasn't talking about a real horse," I said, and took a bite of refried beans. "Or I think the poor thing would be dead by now."

Isaac's mouth twitched a bit. "No, I have a feeling she was using figurative language."

"Figurative language we can't figure out."

"It's way too soon to give up," he said, his

gaze meeting mine, sure and steady, unwavering. I had absolutely no doubt he'd be telling me the same thing six months from now. The man did have a kind of unquenched optimism that could be intimidating. Maybe it was only he knew how far he'd come after the accident that had nearly taken his life, and so he knew better than most people that admitting defeat simply wasn't an option.

But he was right. Because so much had gone on since then, it felt as though I'd discovered the sword years and years earlier. However, the real fact of the matter was that not even a month had elapsed since that fateful day. In books and movies, the heroes could devote their entire lives to finishing their quests, but in the real world, paying the bills and dealing with day-to-day drama—like the mess Dave's untimely death had left behind—meant that sometimes you had to back-burner finding the One Ring.

"I'm not giving up," I said. "I'm just wishing the universe would throw me a bone every once in a while."

He chuckled then. "I know the feeling. But we're on the right track. We just have to keep working away at it."

"Duly noted."

Still wearing a smile, he returned to the chile relleno on his plate, while I ate a few more bites of chicken enchilada. No matter what happened next, I knew I'd think better on a full stomach.

After lunch, Isaac went back to work, while I headed home. The deadline for my latest storyboard project was still over a month away, and yet I knew I should get as much work done as I could...if for no other reason than I needed to have some wiggle room in my schedule in case I had a breakthrough and we needed to go running off to some other remote part of New Mexico to unearth the next clue my bio-mom had left behind. Even though I still didn't know what all these random pieces meant, something was telling me they were part of a larger whole, and maybe—just maybe—if I collected enough of them, I'd finally be able to figure out why she'd gone to such lengths to ensure they would end up in my hands.

It did feel anticlimactic to get out the easel and sketchpad, and to sit down in the living room so I could use the soft light from the big windows there to illuminate my project. Even though dark clouds still lingered over Santa Fe, I had plenty of lighting to work with and knew I wouldn't have to turn on any lamps to see my way.

Because I was leaving the house, I'd put on the protection amulet Isaac had given me before I headed out for our lunch at Tia Maria's. Now I was safely at home, though, I wondered if I should try wearing my bio-mom's turquoise necklace and see whether it had any other visions it would like to share with me. It seemed entirely possible it had been showing me scenes from her life in chronological order, and if that was the case, then maybe this time I'd see exactly where she'd been heading as she drove south on I-25 that bright summer day some thirty years ago.

And since I already had my sketching supplies set out, if I did manage to see something, then I'd be able to get it down quickly instead of scrambling for pen and paper before the images faded completely from my mind.

I'd put the necklace in an inner pocket of my purse before leaving for lunch, mostly because I felt hinky about leaving such a precious relic behind. The house had been locked and the alarm set, of course, and yet it had still seemed safer to have the piece with me. Those protection spells that were wrapped around me at all times didn't just repel magical attacks and demons; they were also very good at making sure muggers stayed far, far away.

Not that getting robbed on the street in broad daylight was a very common occurrence in downtown Santa Fe.

My fingers fumbled with the amulet's clasp for a moment, but then I got it undone and laid the chain and pendant down on the coffee table. A quick trip to the kitchen counter where my purse rested, and I returned to the living room and sat down on the chair in front of my easel. Another moment to get the necklace fastened around my throat, and then it settled against my skin, heavy and still unfamiliar.

The flash came at once. She was sitting on a sofa in a dingy studio apartment that contained a few equally worn-out pieces of furniture. Spread across the banged-up coffee table were sheets and sheets of paper, obviously forms of some kind. Since she wore the same clothes she'd had on when I spied her in the pawn shop and behind the wheel of the car, I guessed this scene must have taken place on the same day.

And while some people might have questioned how I was able to see these things when they were clearly taking place after she'd sold the necklace and therefore should have lost touch with it, I understood she'd maintained a magical connection to the piece, a connection that had little to do with physical contact. Most likely, it was the same kind of enchantment that had been laid on the eyeglasses as well, since once again, the images it had transmitted to me felt almost cinematic, as though seen by some omniscient viewer rather than through my biological mother's eyes.

My own eyes narrowed as I did my best to

focus on the sheets of paper she'd laid out on the coffee table. Most of the print was way too fine for me to make out the words, but at the top of the first sheet was a logo, a stylized heart surrounded by the image of a family holding hands in a circle. Beneath the image was the company name.

Fertility Partners of New Mexico.

Bingo.

This time, the image faded on its own, as if the enchantment somehow knew I'd gotten the information I needed. And while I told myself it had been more than thirty years, and it was entirely possible that Fertility Partners of New Mexico had long since closed up shop the same way Dr. Tillman's clinic in Los Angeles had, I figured that should be easy enough to find out.

My phone was charging on the kitchen peninsula, so I went over and unplugged it, then opened the Safari browser, launched a Google search window, and quickly entered the name of the fertility clinic. It came back on the first hit, with an address in Albuquerque.

Perfect. I touched the link to open Google maps and directions to the clinic, which looked as though it was a bit east of downtown, not too far from the house I'd been renting in Nob Hill.

I wouldn't bother to reflect on the irony of that particular location.

And while maybe I could have just called, I

thought this was the sort of errand that would be better handled in person. After all, it was a lot harder to ignore someone who was standing directly in front of you.

It looked like I was heading to Albuquerque.

Chapter 6
Fertile Imagination

Before I left, though, I sent Isaac a quick text to let him know I was following up on a lead and would be down in Albuquerque for the afternoon. The trip was a calculated risk, just because the first demon my bio-grandmother had sent after me had been able to follow me back to Santa Fe precisely because I'd left the safety of my house and gone to the city to visit Joy, Isaac's cousin and the first friend I'd made here in New Mexico.

However, since nothing suspicious had occurred after I dispatched that second demon a few weeks later, I had to believe my evil grandmother—whoever she was, and wherever she was lurking—didn't actually know where I was living, and when her second minion was banished to hell, she'd been sent back to square one. Otherwise, I had to believe she would have tried once again to have me killed or kidnapped, whichever option best suited her nefarious plans.

I made sure the protection candle was still burning, and I once again placed the amulet around my neck, returning my bio-mom's necklace to the safety of an inner pocket of my purse. A quick recitation of one of the warding spells Isaac had taught me, the one that made me basically invisible to anyone who might mean me harm, and I figured I'd done my due diligence before heading out of Santa Fe and into the greater world.

He sent back a text that said, *Hope it goes well,* but that was all. No admonishments that I needed to stay put until he could accompany me on such an errand, but I hadn't really expected any. Hovering just wasn't Isaac Zamora's style.

But at least now he knew where I was headed, and if he tried to contact me later and couldn't get in touch for some reason, he'd have a better idea of where he needed to look.

Fingers crossed that wouldn't happen, however.

Glad that I'd filled up my SUV's gas tank a few days earlier, I slung my purse over my shoulder and headed out to the garage, arming the alarm as I went. A few minutes later, I was driving south on St. Francis, pointing my Palisade toward I-25.

Since it was the middle of the afternoon, traffic wasn't too bad. Not quite an hour later, I exited the highway and followed the directions from my phone, navigating the confusing tangle of streets until I eventually ended up at Fertility Partners of New Mexico.

It was located in a newish-looking office complex, obviously something that had been built a lot more recently than thirty years ago. Well, there was no law that stated a business had to stay put for the duration of its lifetime.

I got out of the car and sent a quick look around, but the parking lot wasn't terribly full—there was a shiny steel-gray Mercedes in one of the spots near the door, and a few more sedans and SUVs, and that was about it. Also, no one else appeared to be lurking anywhere in the vicinity, which felt like a good thing. Once I'd learned that demons could disguise themselves in human form, it was hard not to be suspicious of any stranger who crossed my path.

No one stopped me from entering the building, however. In the lobby, I took a quick look at the directory mounted to the wall next to the elevator, and determined that Fertility Partners of New Mexico was located on the third floor. A moment of waiting for the car to descend to the ground floor and pick me up, and then I was ascending toward the clinic.

An uneasy feeling roiled in my stomach, and I pulled in a deep breath. I hadn't expected to be this nervous, even though I tried to tell myself the reaction was completely normal. After all, in just a few minutes I might finally learn the identity of the woman who'd given me her red hair and magical gifts, and who had died in that lonely canyon so many years ago.

The elevator stopped at the third floor, and I got out. It appeared there were three suites on this level, with the fertility clinic located to my left. All three suites had glass walls separating them from the foyer, but unlike the other two, where I could see directly into each business's reception area, the ones at Fertility Partners of New Mexico were shielded by blinds that had been closed all the way.

I supposed that made some sense. Anyone coming to a fertility clinic would probably appreciate all the privacy they could get.

Another deep breath, and then I made myself walk through the clinic's door. Immediately ahead of me was a reception desk with a pretty Hispanic woman probably a few years younger than I sitting there. All the chairs in the waiting room were currently unoccupied, and I felt myself relax just a little.

This would definitely be easier without an audience.

The receptionist appeared slightly puzzled as I approached, probably because she didn't recognize me and was most likely doing her best to figure out if I matched up with any of the clinic's appointments that day.

"Hi," I said once I stood directly in front of her. "I was wondering if you could help me."

"Do you have an appointment?" she asked, turning slightly so she could face the computer screen set off to one side.

"No," I responded at once. "But I was hoping you might be able to answer a couple of questions."

Immediately, her expression turned wary. She was one of those women who seemed to have the trick of applying perfect false lashes and cat-eye liner down pat, a look I always found a bit intimidating, as though she'd inherited some sort of girly gene that had been left out of my genetic makeup.

"I'm not sure," she said, her tone as guarded as the look on her face. "What did you need to know?"

"I think the woman who donated the egg my parents used to conceive me donated it here. I wanted to know if there's any way to look up who she was."

The receptionist's perfectly glossed lips tightened. "I'm afraid we can't give out that kind of information. All our donations are done under the strictest confidentiality."

Which was something I'd already guessed, but I had to hope I might be able to wheedle the information out of the woman anyway. That was the main reason why I'd driven down here rather than simply making a phone call.

"I'm not trying to contact her," I said, which was only the truth. My long-dead mother was far past the point where we'd be able to hold a conversation.

Well, unless we attempted a séance or something. I had to wonder why Isaac hadn't mentioned that particular angle when it came to puzzling out my bio-mom's identity. After all the other stuff we'd done, trying to talk to the dead sounded almost quaint.

"I can understand why you'd want to know more," the receptionist said, and at least now she sounded somewhat sympathetic. "But our contracts specifically forbid providing any information regarding our donors to anyone."

"What about for medical reasons?" I asked, trying not to sound too desperate. "I—I'm thinking of starting a family, and I really need to know whether there are any genetic issues I might have inherited from the woman who was my biological mother."

That apparently had been the wrong question to ask, because the receptionist's expression grew shuttered again. "All of our donors are screened for that sort of thing. You can be assured that we don't allow anyone to donate their eggs who might pass along any kind of a hereditary illness."

I supposed I should have thought of that. And here I'd thought I was being so clever, cooking up a lie about starting a family so I'd have a reason to be poking and prying into my bio-mom's history with the clinic.

"Still," I persisted, since I didn't know what else to do, "it would give me a lot of peace of mind to know who she was. I'm not going to ask her for money or attempt to make any kind of contact. I just need a name. That's all."

The receptionist shook her head. "I'm very sorry, but I can't give you that information. There's a reason why we're so strict about such things. Our donors give their eggs because they want to help people who are having trouble conceiving, but that doesn't mean they want to be contacted by those children years later. They have lives and families of their own. Do you understand?"

I did. I really did. And while I wanted to blurt out that the woman in question had been dead for decades and so there was no chance of me showing up on her doorstep, I knew I couldn't tell the receptionist that. She'd want to know how I'd been able to figure out my donor mother was deceased but knew nothing else about her. Put that way, I had to admit the whole thing did sound kind of fishy.

"Yes," I said after a long pause. "I guess so. But I had to try."

"I am sorry," the woman replied. "I'm sure you have absolutely nothing to be concerned about. Like I said, we screen all our donors very carefully. You don't need to worry about any surprises."

No surprises other than discovering the woman who'd contributed to half my genetic makeup had turned out to be a witch, but I had to believe Fertility Partners of New Mexico didn't exactly screen for that sort of thing.

"Thank you," I told the receptionist, even though she really hadn't helped me at all. But policy was policy, and some people could be wheedled and some people just couldn't.

I went back out to the elevator and rode it to the ground floor, extremely glad no one else had gotten on. It would have been hard to try to act pleasant to strangers after that disappointing encounter, but luckily, I wasn't called on to make such an extreme effort.

After I climbed back into my Palisade, I sat there for a moment, wondering if I should run any errands while I was down here in Albuquerque. But no, I definitely wasn't in the mood to go shopping. All I really wanted was to head home to Santa Fe and nurse my disappointment with a glass of wine. I wouldn't even have Isaac to comfort me that evening, since he had a meeting with a local merchants' organization that took place once a month.

Well, I was a big girl. I could handle being alone, even if I would have preferred some company. This whole trip to Albuquerque had been kind of a long shot, anyway.

For all I knew, the clinic didn't even keep records that far back. It was entirely possible that even if the receptionist had been willing to help me, there wouldn't have been anything for her to find.

That thought consoled me a little, even though I guessed deep down that the records probably did exist somewhere, even if they were stuck in a filing cabinet in a storage unit off-site rather than easily accessible on a computer.

The drive home felt excruciatingly slow, mostly because there was definitely more traffic at that hour than there'd been when I'd been on my way to Albuquerque. Eventually, though, I pulled into the driveway and parked my SUV in the garage, then went inside.

As always, the protection candle burned steadily on the kitchen counter. It had done its job, since my trip to the clinic had been spectacularly uneventful...except for the part about being stonewalled and not getting a single piece of information that might help me in my quest to discover my biological mother's identity.

After I'd gone into the kitchen and poured myself some wine, I sat down in the living room and stared at the clock on the mantel for a long time. It was a little after five, a perfectly acceptable time for relaxing with a glass of wine, and yet I still felt as though I needed to do something a little more productive.

Put the necklace back on and see if it could reveal anything else? So far, though, that tactic hadn't yielded much in the way of useful results. I was slowly getting bits and pieces of my mother's activities in the days...or maybe even months... before she'd died, but so far, I still hadn't seen a single thing that had told me definitively who she was.

It might be nice if you'd show me a flash of her driver's license, I thought then with a baleful glance toward my purse, which still held the necklace in an interior pocket. *But no, that would be too easy.*

I had to admit that most people didn't look at their license on a daily basis, which could explain why I hadn't seen it so far. Still, I found myself wishing I'd get a vision of her going to the grocery store or something, just because I had to believe she'd get carded if she tried to buy alcohol.

Except I thought I'd read something during my research about egg donation that said you weren't supposed to drink while taking the various medications prescribed for women going through the donor process, which meant the chances of my bio-mom buying a six-pack of beer during that same period were pretty slim.

Right back to square one.

I sighed and took a sip of wine, glad I didn't have any prescriptions that precluded me from having a drink. Actually, I wasn't on any medications at all, since I didn't think I could count my IUD in that category. One of these days I'd really need to find a doctor here in Santa Fe, but all this business with my mother felt a lot more pressing at the moment, mostly because I kept hoping that if I managed to figure out the mystery she'd left behind, then maybe I'd be able to finally stop looking over my shoulder and worrying about when another demon was going to make an unexpected appearance in my life.

Okay, time for a séance.

And maybe not a real séance, since I was by myself and didn't have anyone else in town who could assist me in attempting such a crazy exploit, but it would still be a way of reaching out, of trying to see whether the spirit of my mother still lingered somewhere in New Mexico. Maybe she'd been the one guiding me all along, and I wasn't really a lodestone at all.

That seemed as good a theory as any, despite Isaac's insistence that I was one of those rare types of witches. On second thought, though, it wasn't too hard to poke holes in my own hypothesis. After all, if I really had only been following the clues left behind by my bio-mom rather than having some inner instinct guide me, that still didn't explain how I'd been able to find exactly the right props for whatever show I'd been working on, or how I was the one person my friends came to when they needed exactly the right present for a special occasion. Apparently, my *chi* had been pretty well blocked back then, thanks to first being surrounded by my mother's negative energies and then by Dave's, but that blockage hadn't been enough to prevent me from attracting the items I needed in my life.

Well, I'd worry about all that later.

I was kind of fuzzy on how exactly one went about conducting a solo séance, but I thought it couldn't hurt to light some more candles, and to turn on the gas for the fireplace so I'd have the calming flicker of flames in the background to help set the mood. There were some tealights and votive holders in one of the kitchen cupboards, and I went and fetched them, then brought them back to the living room and set them on the coffee table.

By that point, dusk was starting to fall. I closed the blinds and turned on a few lamps, since I figured I didn't need an audience for my attempt at reaching out to the afterlife. The house felt a lot cozier after I was done, and I hoped my warmly serene surroundings would also help my mental state.

I sat back down on the sofa, belatedly

wondering whether I should be doing all this at the dining room table rather than here in the living room. Then I decided the heck with it—this wasn't going to be your standard séance by any stretch of the imagination, and so I figured it probably didn't matter where I was sitting. Besides, this had always been my favorite room in the house, despite my ex dropping dead from a demon-induced heart attack in this very space only a few weeks earlier.

After lighting all the votives—and one of the sandalwood incense cones I'd picked up at Isaac's shop a while back—I let myself sit there and breathe in and out for a few minutes, doing my best to calm my racing thoughts and make myself focus on the room where I sat, the welcoming environment I'd done my best to create. I actually did start to feel a bit better, some of the jangly energy I'd brought home from my disappointing trip to Albuquerque gradually beginning to fade away.

Because I had no idea how to address her—every attempt so far to learn my biological mother's name had been stymied, and calling her "Mom" just felt weird—I instead fixed an image of her in my mind, hoping I might try summoning her that way. It had made me happy to see her driving along in her pale green Buick, with the wind blowing in her long copper hair. I'd long ago cut mine fairly short, in a longish curly bob that barely touched my collarbones, just because with a lifestyle like mine, having long hair was too much work. Now, though, I wondered if I should grow it out. That long red hair had looked great on my bio-mom, and since our features were so similar, I guessed it would work on me as well.

Focus, Penny.

Right.

Once again, I fixed the image of her in my mind, the way she was singing along with the radio, how her fingers tapped on the steering wheel in time with the beat. I called out then, not with any words, but with all the need I'd held in my heart, the need to know who she'd been and what had happened to her.

And...nothing. I tried my best not to pay attention to time passing, despite the ticking of the clock on the mantel. It wasn't as though I had anywhere I needed to be, and so it really didn't matter how long it might take me to establish some kind of contact with the woman I was seeking. I just needed to be Zen about this, even if most people, when asked, would have said I was probably one of the least Zen people they'd ever met.

Maybe it was stupid to attempt this without Isaac's guidance. I had no reason to believe he knew much about holding séances or acting as a medium, but at least he knew what he was doing when it came to all things magical. And I also had to admit he was much better at remaining focused, of not allowing his brain to get in the way of whatever needed to be done.

I, on the other hand, didn't seem to be much good at any of this. Well, except for killing demons, but even that had been a fluke. Without the enchanted sword my biological mother had left for me to find, I would have been up shit creek without the proverbial paddle during that little encounter.

Okay, desperate times called for desperate measures.

I got up from the couch and went into the kitchen, then got out the half-drunk bottle of chardonnay that sat on the bottom shelf of the fridge. After pouring some into one of my stemless tumblers, I headed back to the living room, took a few swallows of wine, and hoped the mild infusion of alcohol would help me relax and allow my mind to make contact with the plane where my mother's soul now lived.

All this assumed, of course, that there was such a thing as life after death. Isaac hadn't talked much about those sorts of matters, but I had to believe that if demons and magic were real, then something like heaven and hell also had to exist, even if they didn't take the same form that people commonly assumed they did.

Time to try again.

I need your help, I thought, doing my best to

direct the mental words outward to the universe. *I don't know where to look next. You've been trying to tell me something, I know, but I can't figure out what the riddle is supposed to mean.*

And then I swallowed some more wine, figuring if nothing else, I could always use a little extra muscle relaxant.

A blink, and she was standing there in front of me.

Every muscle in my body stiffened with shock, even as I realized what I saw now was only an apparition, or maybe even a figure conjured by my own brain from my own need. She was transparent, and I could see the outline of the fireplace right through her, the flames seeming to leap somewhere around her midsection.

She was shorter than I'd expected, telling me I'd probably gotten my height from my father. But the copper-red hair was the same, and the faintly amused lift to her full lips. Because she was so see-through, like the image of a woman printed on chiffon, I couldn't really see her eye color. I knew it was gray, though, gray with just the slightest hint of green, reminding me of new leaves seen through a fog.

Her mouth opened, but the words I heard next rang inside my head rather than reaching my ears.

You already know everything you need to know. The answer will come to you soon.

And then she was gone.

I blinked and looked around in some desperation, as if an addled part of my brain thought she might have hidden herself behind the sofa or something. But no, there was no sign of the ghostly figure who'd been standing in front of the fireplace only a few minutes earlier.

For all I knew, I'd conjured her entirely from my own anguished need to know what was going on, and nothing more.

So, I supposedly already had everything I needed?

Yeah, right.

My cell phone rang then, and I startled. It was a little past five-thirty by that point, and so Isaac would still be at work. I had no idea who might be calling me, since Brooke Knowles, the attorney who was handling my estate issues with Dave, probably wouldn't be working at that hour. Plus, it sounded as though my father had a pretty packed schedule that day and so wouldn't have much opportunity to call, even if there had been a reason for making contact so soon after seeing me.

Only one way to find out.

I got up from the couch and hurried over to retrieve my phone from where it sat in its charging station on the kitchen peninsula. The number wasn't one I recognized, one with a 202 area code.

Wasn't that somewhere on the East Coast?

Mystified, I lifted the phone to my ear. "Hello?"

A male voice, unfamiliar, but crisp and businesslike. "Penny Briggs?"

"Yes," I said cautiously. Because I'd immediately listed my number with the national "do not call" registry, I didn't get a lot of spam. All the same, it never hurt to be wary.

"I'm Special Agent Ted Highsmith with the FBI. I'm calling to let you know we've determined the identity of the woman who went missing thirty-two years ago."

Chapter 7
Ride a Wild Pony

I t was a good thing the dining room table and its accompanying chairs were only a few feet away, because after receiving that piece of astonishing news, my knees felt like rubber and I knew I needed to sit down or risk collapsing on the floor right then and there. Yes, I'd initiated this search a while back—or rather, Isaac had, by reaching out to his cousin who worked for the Santa Fe P.D.—but I'd honestly begun to think nothing would ever come of it.

The answer will come to you soon.

Talk about timing. Were ghosts really that omniscient, or was this a case of simple dumb luck and nothing else?

"You found her?" I managed. "Who was she?"

"Her name was Mina Elizabeth Powers," Agent Highsmith replied. "Age twenty-two, from Boulder, Colorado. She disappeared in May 1990. Her mother first reported her missing, and told the police in Boulder that they'd had a disagreement and she'd left town. There was quite the manhunt, but no one ever reported seeing her. About ten years later, some hikers found human remains in Red Rock State Park outside Gallup, New Mexico. Eventually, dental records identified those remains as belonging to Ms. Powers. Her family was notified, and Ms. Powers' remains were sent back to Boulder."

Red Rock State Park. Gallup, New Mexico.

Of course.

Ride the roan—a roan was a red horse. A horse that galloped, apparently. I still had no idea what the patriarch's tears were, but I was willing to bet a large chunk of Dave's life insurance money that they had to be hidden somewhere near Gallup.

Part of me wanted to laugh, but I had a feeling that sort of reaction wouldn't go over very well with the brisk-sounding federal agent, considering what we'd just been discussing.

"Thank you so much, Agent Highsmith," I said. "This really helps me out a lot."

"No problem at all," he replied. "I'm sorry it took so long to get back to you, but this was an old case, and one that was solved a long time ago, so it took a bit of digging." A pause, and then he went on in a slightly different tone, "If you don't mind my asking, why was this case so important to you?"

Part of me wanted to make up a story on the spot, but I felt weird about lying to a federal agent. On the other hand, there was no reason he needed to know the complete truth.

"I think we might be related somehow," I said, figuring that statement should be vague enough to be mostly harmless. "But everything I was trying to track down turned into a total dead end, so this really gives me the missing pieces I was looking for."

"I'm sorry it couldn't be better news," he replied.

"That's all right," I told him. "I mean, it all happened a long time ago. But now I can have some closure."

"Glad to help," Agent Highsmith said. "You have a good evening, Ms. Briggs."

And the call ended.

Definitely a "just the facts, ma'am" kind of guy, but I was all right with that. In fact, I was glad he'd ended the call, because I wanted to reach out to Isaac and let him know what I'd just learned.

Except it was now exactly six, which meant he'd be busy closing up the shop and getting ready to head over to his meeting. I allowed myself an inner groan. Why did he have to have a meeting tonight of all nights?

I consoled myself with the reminder that those meetings didn't tend to run very late, according to Isaac, and so I could call him around eight-thirty and see if he was available. Worst case scenario, I'd leave a voicemail and let him know he could call me as late as midnight if need be.

But just because Isaac was otherwise occupied didn't mean I was dead in the water. I now knew my bio-mom's name, which meant I could try to do some digging on my own.

Unfortunately, some quick internet searches—searches I performed using a VPN and an anonymous browser, since I didn't really want Google to know what I was up to in case those very searches triggered some kind of alarm set by my evil maternal grandmother—didn't pull up anything about my particular Mina Powers. It wasn't the world's most common name, but I found a woman with the same exact name in Raleigh, North Carolina, another in Vancouver, British Columbia, and yet another in London, England. Clearly, none of them were the woman who'd perished in Red Rock State Park more than thirty years earlier, and while there might have been police bulletins about the missing twenty-two-year-old, it had been so long ago that they hadn't been properly indexed in any way that appeared to be findable by Duck Duck Go.

Not that I intended to give up so quickly. I

picked up my phone and sent my father a quick text.

Hey, Dad, it said, *could you give me the contact info for the P.I. you used to investigate Dr. Lightman's fertility clinic? I have something else I want him to work on.*

The reply came back fairly quickly, telling me that at least I hadn't interrupted my father during dinner. *Sure—I'll send it over now. What's this about?*

Although I didn't think he would be upset about me wanting to learn more regarding my bio-mom, I also didn't feel quite right sending that information via text. *Something connected to that other matter,* I responded. *Just doing some follow-up.*

Because my father had learned a thing or two over the years about being discreet, he didn't press the issue. *No problem,* he sent back. *Give me a minute to get his information.*

Thanks, Dad.

I waited for my phone to ping again, which it did only about thirty seconds later. *Don Tanner, 310-555-2287.*

Awesome.

I copied the information into my phone's contacts, then wrote back, *Thanks again. I'll let you know what I find.*

Sounds good.

We ended the convo then, and I glanced over at the clock. Now it was a bit past six, meaning it was only a little after five in L.A. Somehow, I didn't think a private investigator would be too concerned about those five minutes or so. I had to believe that line of work didn't exactly involve working a standard forty-hour week.

And although the coward in me would have much preferred to simply send a text, I guessed it would look a lot better if I actually called. At least this Don Tanner person already had a professional relationship with my father, so it wouldn't be as though I was calling him totally out of the blue.

Still, I figured a little liquid courage to help me with my phone anxiety couldn't hurt.

Phone in hand, I went back to the couch and sat down, then had a swallow or two of chardonnay to bolster me. Before I could lose my nerve, I navigated to my contacts list, went down to Don Tanner's entry, and touched the phone icon to make the call.

His phone rang several times, and I wondered if I'd been off the mark when it came to speculating about whether he worked odd hours. But then the call connected, and I heard a pleasant man's voice say, "Tanner Investigations."

He sounded younger than I'd expected. For some reason, my brain had been telling me that all private investigators must be gravel-voiced men in their fifties, which obviously wasn't the truth in this particular case. In fact, Mr. Tanner sounded like the sort of guy who might have spent the morning surfing before he headed off to photograph cheating spouses or whatever it was that P.I.s generally did with their days.

"Hi, Don," I said, and then wondered if I should have addressed him more formally, even though it felt weird to call someone "Mr." who sounded like he was around my own age of thirty-two. "My name is Penny Briggs. I'm Gerald Briggs's daughter."

"Hi, Penny," Don said. If he was at all offended by my casual use of his first name, you definitely couldn't tell from the friendly tone of his reply. "What can I do for you?"

"I was hoping you could do a little digging about a woman who died more than thirty years ago. I have her full name and her hometown, but I can't really give you any more information than that."

His quick response reassured me somewhat. "Oh, that should definitely be enough to get me started," he said. "Do you want to come into the office so we can discuss the case further? I'm in Santa Monica."

I couldn't help smiling a little, even though he obviously couldn't see my expression. "That might be a little tough," I replied. "I'm in Santa Fe right now."

"Santa Fe, New Mexico?"

To be fair, there was a Santa Fe Springs in Southern California, and there were several other Santa Fes scattered around the globe, so the question wasn't as silly as it might have seemed on the surface. "Yes, in New Mexico," I said. "I was hoping there might be a secure way to send you the information."

"Of course," he said at once. "I have a private server I use for storing documents. I'll need to send you a contract first, but once we have that settled, I'll give you a login and you can copy whatever documents you have over there."

I almost told him I didn't have any documents at all, but I figured I could write down everything I knew about Mina Powers in a text file and then upload that. It should be enough to get the ball rolling.

"No problem," I said. "You can email me the contract."

After I gave him my email address, he said, "Great. I'm out of the office right now, but I'll send that over first thing in the morning—unless this is time critical, in which case, I'll try to send it to you later tonight."

As much as I wanted to get him to work as soon as possible, I knew there wasn't a huge amount of urgency here, not when we were trying to investigate a woman who'd died decades ago.

"Tomorrow morning is fine," I assured him.

"Thanks," he replied. "Have a good evening."

An echo of what Agent Highsmith had said to me a few minutes earlier.

I had to hope both of them would be right.

As it turned out, I did feel much better after my phone call with Don Tanner. At least I could feel as though I'd taken some steps to find out more about my mother and the mysterious family she'd come from. The rest of it would just have to wait a bit. After all, I had no idea how long it would take Don to even begin digging up that information.

So, I had a quickie dinner of some grilled chicken tossed with olive oil, fettuccine, and parmesan, and went ahead and finished the bottle of wine as I ate in front of the TV. Feeling a lot more mellow than I'd been when the evening started, I paused the show a little past eight-thirty, and picked up my phone so I could call Isaac.

To my relief, he answered right away. "Penny. Everything quiet over there?"

"It's extremely chill," I replied. "But I wanted to let you know I finally heard from your cousin's friend in the FBI. He actually found my bio-mom

—her name was Mina Powers, and she lived in Boulder, Colorado."

"That's great news," he said, and I could tell from the surprise and relief in his tone that he genuinely was happy for me. "Colorado? Then it makes sense that she would have come through New Mexico, would have used our state to hide the sword and the riddle."

"Oh, it gets better," I told him, even as I experienced a warm little flush of happiness at the way he'd described New Mexico as "our" state. Clearly, he didn't think I was going anywhere. Doing my best to sound brisk and no-nonsense, I went on, "Mina Powers' remains were found in Red Rock State Park. I guess that's outside Gallup somewhere?"

I couldn't see him, of course, but I got the feeling Isaac smacked his forehead right then. "Of course," he said. "I should have thought of Red Rock park. I haven't been there since I was a kid, but—"

"It's all right," I cut in. "If I'd just had the sense to Google 'red rock new mexico,' I would have found it right away. I guess I didn't think the solution would be so...literal."

"And so the 'red roan' from the riddle is probably the park outside Gallup," Isaac said next.

"I think so," I said. "But we won't know for sure until we go check it out."

A pause, and he replied, "Another road trip?"

"I guess so," I said. When I'd driven to New Mexico from California, the leg of the journey from Gallup to Albuquerque had felt interminable, but that was probably mostly because I'd been on the road for almost two days by that point, and I'd just wanted to get to my destination and get out of the damn car. But now I was in Santa Fe, adding another hour to the journey. Gallup was about three hours one way, just far enough that it would probably be better to book a hotel room, especially since I had no idea how long it would take to find those patriarch's tears, whatever they turned out to be. And because Isaac hadn't responded right away, I asked, "Will you be able to take some time off work? I know it's asking a lot, especially since you had to close down for a couple of days just a few weeks ago to go running off to Cimarron, but—"

"It's fine," he broke in, but gently. "This time of year is pretty quiet, since the Christmas rush won't start for me for a few more weeks."

Christmas. It was hard to believe that it was now only about five weeks away, but I couldn't let myself forget it was looming out there on the horizon, just waiting to appear and suck all the oxygen out of the room. I still hadn't been able to decide whether or not to go back to California for at least part of the holidays, even if I managed to stay here in New Mexico for the big day itself rather than give in to my mother's pressure to return home.

Home. There was a joke. The rented house where I was currently living felt far more like home than my parents' big house in Pacific Palisades ever had.

"Okay," I said. "Then I'll look for a place to stay, and in the meantime, you can make any preparations you need to do for closing the shop."

"It won't be much," Isaac said, a wry note entering his voice. "Mostly, I just need to print out a sign saying that I'll be closed until next Monday, then head down to the store and tape it to the door."

I hadn't told him how much time I'd expected this to take, mostly because I really didn't have any idea. Four days sounded like a lot, but I guessed he was just being cautious. If we wrapped this up quickly, he could take down the sign as soon as we got back, and most of the tourists who frequented the downtown area would be none the wiser.

And if it turned out we needed more than four days?

Well, I supposed we'd cross that bridge when we came to it.

"Sounds good," I said. "Pick you up tomorrow around nine-thirty?"

As I spoke, I wondered if I was shooting myself

in the foot with that timing. What if Don Tanner hadn't sent over his contract before then?

I told myself I'd bring my laptop along, and tether it to my cell phone at the earliest opportunity so I could download any important emails, including the one with the contract. Yes, I could do that same thing on my phone, but I would much rather fill out any paperwork on the laptop than try to navigate a .pdf on a cell phone.

"See you then," Isaac replied, and added, "This is a great development, Penny. I can tell we're getting close."

Close to what, I wasn't sure. But I supposed we'd find that out once we got to Gallup.

"I hope so," I said. "See you in the morning."

We ended the call there, and I went into the office so I could once again navigate to Booking.com and see what I might find for the two of us at such short notice. At least Gallup had a little more to offer than Cimarron had, although I wouldn't call any of its accommodations exactly four-star. But the Hampton Inn looked clean and had decent ratings. Most importantly, it had two rooms available.

Maybe one day I wouldn't need to worry about getting Isaac and me separate rooms, but that day definitely hadn't come yet.

I booked the rooms for three nights, and went ahead and started getting some clothes together for the trip. Nothing fancy, just jeans and thermal tops and a couple of jackets...and those damn work boots of mine. I really should have used some of my downtime to head over to REI and get myself a pair of real hiking boots, but I hadn't thought I'd be heading out into the wild so soon after our last little jaunt to find the breadcrumbs Mina Powers had left behind.

Well, at least this time I wouldn't have to worry about tripping over the *Fool's Gold* film crew the way we had when we'd gone to Cimarron, following the clues on the key I'd found in that mountain outside Taos. They were filming in various spots around the state, but Gallup hadn't been on any of the location lists I'd seen for the show, so we should be in the clear.

No, all Isaac and I now needed to worry about was what we might find in Gallup...and whether it would provide the clues we needed, or merely add to the continuing riddle of my biological mother's death.

Chapter 8
A Galloping Horse

I went ahead and packed the compass along with the sword—no way would I leave that shiny blade behind with both Isaac and me out of town—but I had my doubts whether the compass was actually going to provide any real assistance. As soon as I'd finalized our travel plans the night before, I'd gone and dug the compass out of the box where I'd been keeping it along with the rest of my meager jewelry collection, hoping that maybe now I had a real destination, it would have come to life again, would be pointing southwest where Gallup lay in relation to Santa Fe.

But no, the compass's needle was still stubbornly fixed on due north, the way it had been ever since I'd found the sword and the riddle buried deep in that mountain outside Cimarron. If it ever planned to wake up again, it sure didn't show any signs of it at the moment.

Better to have it on hand, though, just in case.

A scrim of high clouds covered the sky as I went to pick up Isaac that morning, dulling the usual New Mexico bright blue and making me wonder whether our venture had any true chance of success. Logically, I knew the weather had very little to do with our quest—well, unless we got an unseasonably early snowstorm, which I prayed wouldn't happen—but I still would have preferred to have bright sunny skies, something that would have felt like a happy omen of success.

However, I cheered up as soon as I arrived at Isaac's house and found him waiting for me, one bag packed...and his wheelchair conspicuously absent.

"You don't want to take your chair?" I asked as we headed out to my SUV.

Isaac shook his head, then tossed his duffle bag into the back of the Palisade. He was leaning on his crutches, but I could tell he was barely putting any weight on them, and mostly seemed to have them there because he figured he might as well bring them along. "I haven't used it in almost two weeks now, so I thought I'd live dangerously."

For a second or two, I considered protesting that maybe it would be better to bring the chair, just in case. But since he was a grown man who'd been managing his health issues just fine long before I arrived on the scene, I decided it was better not to say anything. Well, nothing more than, "That's great news. And it does free up some space in the back, just in case those patriarch's tears turn out to be bulky."

"Don't forget about the circle of iron," he quipped, then climbed into the Palisade's passenger seat.

No, I hadn't forgotten about that part of the riddle, although I'd been paying more attention to those tears because they were mentioned first...and also because I couldn't figure out what the heck they were supposed to be. A circle of iron seemed a little more self-explanatory.

"I guess we'll just have to hope they're both carry-on size," I replied before following his lead and getting into my own seat.

Since I'd filled the Palisade's gas tank before driving over here, there was nothing to delay us as I cut through downtown and eventually pulled onto southbound I-25. By that point, the morning rush was mostly over, and so we made good time, getting past Albuquerque and onto the open highway heading west in less than an hour.

"We should get to Gallup around lunch," I said as we passed the Route 66 Casino with its gaudy neon sign. "I'm hoping once I'm there, I'll get sort of a ping as to where we're supposed to go next. We might as well explore a bit, since our hotel room won't be ready until after three."

"Well, we can eat first," Isaac replied. "We'll need to use Yelp to find something, though—I don't know Gallup very well."

Apparently not, or he might have told me right off the bat that Red Rock State Park was probably our best bet when it came to locating the place where my mother had met her end at a demon's hands. But no, that wasn't fair. Just because Isaac was far more skilled with magic than I would probably ever be, it still didn't mean he was omniscient, or could immediately find his way through even the thorniest puzzle.

Besides, maybe we were coming here now because this was exactly when we were supposed to solve this part of the riddle. As Isaac had told me on more than one occasion, sometimes we just had to trust that the universe knew what it was doing.

Also, the skies cleared as we headed west, and soon enough, we had serene blue overhead. This might not have been the prettiest time of year to be traveling through these parts, since the autumn color was mostly gone and the wild grasses yellow and tired-looking, but the geology of the state itself was striking enough, with the impressive bulk of Mount Taylor just outside Grants on one side, and rolling hills and mysterious canyons on the other.

And yes, there was even some red rock as we

got closer to Gallup, the formations' rusty outlines striking against the sheared-off tops of the mesas. By that point, we'd been driving for almost three hours, and I was glad to know our destination wasn't too far off.

Isaac pulled out his phone, presumably so he could root around on Yelp and see if he could find anything promising. "There's a Mediterranean place that sounds good," he said after a moment. "Want to try that?"

The suggestion sounded great to me. I loved the food in Santa Fe, and New Mexican cuisine in general, but so far I hadn't found any restaurants in town that could satisfy my cravings for kabob. "Definitely," I said. "It would be a nice change of pace."

"Okay. Then I'll let the Yelp directions nav us in."

Which they did, guiding us off the interstate and down Route 66. I had to admit the restaurant didn't look very prepossessing from the outside, its architecture a throwback to a 1960s diner, with the added dubious bonus of train tracks directly across the street, but the wonderful aroma that hit my nose as soon as we opened the door told me we'd probably made a good choice.

True, the interior of the restaurant pretty much matched the outside, with its industrial-looking ceiling tiles and plain-vanilla furniture, but everything appeared scrupulously clean, and since almost every table was full, I had to guess that none of the locals cared too much about the ambience.

A pretty girl in her early twenties wearing a head scarf guided us to one of the two remaining tables and handed us some menus, which Isaac and I both gratefully accepted. I didn't know how much of a breakfast he'd had, but I'd only eaten a couple of pieces of toast before leaving the house, and was looking forward to something a bit more substantial than a few slices of bread.

After our waitress showed up and took our drink orders—iced tea for both of us, since the restaurant didn't appear to serve alcohol...probably just as well—Isaac returned his attention to me.

"Feel anything?"

I didn't bother to ask him exactly what I was supposed to be feeling. While it had been interesting to get off the highway and drive around a little bit in a completely unfamiliar town, I hadn't sensed anything out of the ordinary about this place, hadn't gotten an "a-ha" moment or anything that might tell me we were on the right track here.

"Nothing," I said. "Maybe my instincts will kick in after I get some food in my stomach."

He sent me a wry smile at that remark but didn't say anything, as the waitress returned right then with our iced teas. We both placed our orders —chicken kabob for me and beef shawarma for him—and then settled against our seats to enjoy the iced tea and wait for our food to arrive.

"The compass?" he said briefly, and I lifted my shoulders.

"I don't know," I replied. "I mean, when I checked it this morning, it was still stuck pointing north, but I haven't looked at it recently."

"Maybe you should."

At least I'd had the presence of mind to transfer the thing into one of my hoodie's pockets before leaving the house that morning. I'd also hung both the protection amulet and Mina Powers' turquoise necklace around my throat, mostly because it had seemed important to have both of them with me, even if the combo looked a little strange. Luckily, I wasn't trying to impress anyone, so I figured it didn't really matter if my accessorizing was a little wacky.

I fished the compass out of my pocket and glanced down at it. To my surprise, the needle actually had begun to move again—not quickly, but enough to prove it wasn't at a complete standstill.

"Look," I said, and handed the golden device across the table to Isaac.

Brows lifting faintly in surprise, he stared at the compass's face. "It seems the change in venue must have woken it up."

"I guess so," I replied, then shrugged. "But since it doesn't seem to be pointing anywhere in particular, I'm not sure how much help it's going to be."

"Give it time," Isaac told me, which was about what I'd figured he would say. Impatient, he was not. "It's been dormant for a while. Maybe it just needs some more time to recalibrate."

Hopefully, not too much time. Previously, it had taken days and days to get its act together and actually point somewhere useful, but we were only going to be in Gallup for three nights. And yes, Isaac had told me he could get his brother Diego to head over to the shop and change the sign in the window if it turned out we needed to extend our fact-finding mission. Still, I didn't think it would be fair to keep him here for an open-ended span of time. He had a business to run.

Actually, so did I. Or at least, I had a freelance project I needed to complete, so I also couldn't be running around in the wilderness for forty days and forty nights, or however long it might take to find those patriarch's tears.

Well, no point in borrowing trouble before it even arrived. The compass had woken up, and I should take that as a good sign. Everything else would fall into place sooner or later.

I hoped.

I made an affirmative sound in reply to Isaac's comment, and he got the message. From there, we talked about getting settled in at the hotel, and how much daylight we'd have to go poking around after that.

"We might as well drive out to the state park and see what we can find," he said. "Even if we only have an hour or so. Maybe our little friend"— he made the slightest of nods toward the compass, which I'd returned to my pocket—"will do better once it's closer to the place we'll be exploring."

That sounded like as good a plan as any. "Here's hoping," I replied, and grinned as I lifted my iced tea so he could clink his own glass against it.

The food arrived soon after that, and proved to be as good as all those Yelp reviews had stated. I found my outlook on life improving the more chicken kabob and rice and pita I consumed. If nothing else, this would be some good fuel for whatever exploring we ended up doing.

It was not quite one-thirty by the time we headed back out to my SUV, far too early to check into our hotel at the east end of town. However, it seemed Isaac had a plan to fill up the time, because he nodded toward the turquoise necklace once we were back inside the Palisade and said, "I thought we might want to ask around about that, too."

"Mina's necklace?" I returned, a bit startled. It felt much easier to think of her by her given name, rather than as my biological mother, and so I'd already started using it as much as I could. "But wouldn't she have bought it in Colorado, if that's where she came from?"

"She might have bought it there," Isaac said easily, not at all put off by my question. "But I doubt it was made there. Gallup is a huge center for Native American art and jewelry, and a lot of the people working in the stores here are experts. Are there any maker's marks on the back of the necklace?"

I knew there were, because I'd inspected the piece closely after bringing it home. It had the standard ".925" mark, indicating it was sterling silver, but there was also a small stamp that looked like a tiny "B" in the center of an elongated diamond. "Yes," I said, and then described what I'd seen stamped into the silver. "You think it means something?"

"It might," he replied. "If nothing else, knowing who made the piece might tell us something about the route it traveled before coming into Mina Powers' possession. It obviously has a strength of its own, or it wouldn't have been able to send you such clear visions."

Well, I thought that point was highly debatable. I didn't know whether the necklace had anything to do with the visions at all, other than having Mina's own strong magic surrounding it and penetrating the very metal and the stone itself, giving it the ability to show me what she'd wanted me to see.

But I had to admit I was curious about where the piece had come from, so I wasn't going to argue. We still had an hour to kill before heading over to the hotel, and that certainly wasn't enough time to start wandering around Red Rock State Park.

So, I followed Isaac's directions to a shop farther downtown. Why he chose that one out of all the stores in Gallup that sold Native American jewelry, I didn't know—it seemed there was a place hawking turquoise jewelry on every corner—but I dutifully pulled over and parked on the street, then got out. I had to wait a bit for Isaac to navigate his way out of the SUV and tuck his crutches under his arms, but soon enough, we were walking into the store in question.

Truthfully, I'd seen some pretty spectacular shops in Santa Fe, but even those stores hadn't prepared me for what I saw now. On every side were display cases filled with eye-popping specimens of Native American jewelry, from huge squash-blossom necklaces studded with gorgeous chunks of sky-blue turquoise to sterling concho belts and tray after tray of rings and cuffs and pendants.

Almost as soon as we entered, an older man, probably Navajo, with his elegant cheekbones and sleek gray-streaked black hair, approached us. "Can I help you find something?" he asked.

"Actually, we were hoping you might be able to identify the necklace my friend here is wearing," Isaac replied.

I tried not to get too bent at his use of the word "friend." Our relationship was far too complicated to try quantifying to a perfect stranger. Instead, I reached up and undid the clasp, then handed the necklace over to the shopkeeper.

He took it from me, night-dark eyes narrowing as he studied the unusual design, the gorgeous chunk of spiderweb turquoise that was the focal point of the piece. When he turned it over to study the back, he gave a knowing nod.

"Nelson Begay," he said. "I thought that as soon as I saw it, but the hallmark here just proves my hunch."

And he pointed at the little "B" in its delicate diamond-shaped frame.

"Navajo?" Isaac asked, and the shopkeeper nodded.

"Yes. He passed away about five years ago. This is a very valuable piece, quite collectible." The old man's eyes narrowed slightly as he glanced over at me. "Where did you get it?"

"At a store in Santa Fe," I said. "But I think it came there via a pawn shop."

The shopkeeper's expression grew somehow

sad at that revelation. "Yes, it probably would have fetched a good price, especially if the person who owned the pawn shop knew anything about the artist who made it."

"We were hoping you might have known when and where it was made," Isaac put in.

Once again, the shopkeeper turned the necklace over in his hands, studying the design. "This would have been one of Nelson's older pieces, probably made in the late 1980s or early '90s. He was experimenting with design more back then and often used animal motifs, especially ravens and other birds. Luckily, because his work is so collectible, it's catalogued more than that of many other local artists. Do you mind waiting a few minutes? I'll need to go through my catalogue collection and see what I can find."

"Take as long as you need," I said quickly, even as I shot Isaac a hopeful glance. Was it really possible the shopkeeper at the trading post would be able to tell us exactly where and when the necklace had been first sold?

Isaac's expression was encouraging, even though he remained silent as the shop owner went through a door behind the counter where we'd been standing, obviously access to a storage room of some sort. There didn't seem to be anyone else working in the shop right then, although I guessed the security cameras mounted everywhere would provide plenty of deterrent to anyone who might try to help themselves to a ten-finger discount while the shopkeeper was out of sight.

A couple of minutes went by, during which I inspected the items in the case nearest us. In fact, there was a gorgeous ring set with a piece of spiderweb turquoise that almost exactly matched the necklace we were investigating. I'd never been much for rings, except my plain white gold wedding band—now stashed in a pouch in my sock drawer, since I'd stopped wearing it months earlier —but now I wondered whether I should get the turquoise ring I'd just spied. It would be nice to have a matching piece for the necklace, and it would also be a way of saying thank-you to the shopkeeper for all the help he'd given us.

Almost as though my thoughts had summoned him, the man emerged from the storeroom holding what looked like a large-format trade paperback of some sort, although the title seemed to indicate it was actually a catalogue from a gallery called Turquoise Trail.

"I thought the necklace seemed familiar," the man told us as he spread the catalogue open on the counter so Isaac and I could take a closer look. "It was a featured piece in the spring collection at a gallery that specializes in Native American art and jewelry."

"Where's the gallery located?" Isaac asked.

"Denver," the shopkeeper replied, and I could hardly contain the burst of excitement that pulsed through me at his reply. After all, it didn't seem too outrageous to think Mina Powers must have seen the necklace and bought it for herself, since Boulder and Denver were practically right next door to each other. Also, if the raven motif was typical of Nelson Begay's work from the late '80s or early '90s, then the timeline worked out pretty closely as well.

"Do you know who bought it?" I said, doing my best to hide the eagerness in my tone. I probably wasn't too successful, however.

The man shook his head at once, though, quelling some of my enthusiasm. "No, this is only a catalogue of what the gallery was offering that season. I'd say you could try contacting Turquoise Trail to find out more, but I doubt their records go that far back."

No, probably not. We were talking about a piece of jewelry that must have been sold thirty-two or thirty-three years ago, not an item from last season or something.

Despite that minor setback, I was feeling pretty good about the situation. After all, we now knew a lot more than we had when we walked through the shop door some fifteen minutes earlier.

"That's fine," I said. "I just figured I'd ask." Then I smiled and added, pointing to the piece in question, "Could I see that spiderweb turquoise ring in the case here? I think it would go really well with my necklace."

"That it would," the shop owner agreed, now looking much more cheerful. "You have a good eye —that's another of Nelson's pieces, although a later one. Still, they're such a close match that I have to wonder if they were both sourced from the same material, even if they were made years apart. Here you are."

And he unlocked the case, pulled out the ring, and set it in my palm. I lifted it with my other hand and tried it on, discovering that it fit the middle finger of my right hand perfectly. As the shop-keeper had pointed out, the ring was a different style from the necklace, far less elaborate, with a rope-style bezel and a few round dots of silver deco-rating the side of the bezel before it moved down into the ring's split shank.

But I loved the simplicity of it, the way it contrasted with the necklace and yet enhanced its beauty at the same time. And I also loved the way the ring looked on my hand, how I could feel its weight but somehow knew it would never get in the way.

"It's perfect," I said. "I'll take it." Without even bothering to ask how much the ring was, I pulled out my Visa debit card and handed it over to the man.

He might have blinked. However, all he said was, "Wonderful. Would you like to wear it, or do you want me to box it up for you?"

My answer was immediate. "Oh, I'll wear it."

The ring was fairly expensive—not that it could have given any of my mother's Tiffany or Bulgari pieces a run for their money—but I didn't care. I didn't spend money on myself very often, especially on frivolous stuff like jewelry. And I couldn't quite shake the feeling that the ring had been waiting for me, waiting for the right person to come along and give it a good home.

Through all of this, Isaac had remained quiet, watching as I took care of the transaction and then folded the receipt for the ring into my wallet. Once we were back outside, however, he said quietly, "The ring called to you."

I angled an amused glance up at him. "More lodestone stuff?"

"If you want to look at it that way," he returned, unperturbed. "But clearly, it was meant to be with you, to be with the necklace. I'm glad you found it."

I'd thought pretty much the same thing. However, I couldn't help asking, "So, you don't think I'm crazy for spending four hundred bucks on a turquoise ring?"

"No. If buying it caused financial hardship, then maybe it's something you should have

thought about more before spending the money."
He shrugged, waiting as I got out my fob to unlock
the Palisade. "But since that's not the case, it's clear
enough to me that you were meant to have it."

Maybe I was. I'd had so many weird things
happen to me over the past month or so, I couldn't
really argue that serendipity and coincidence
weren't a thing. If the universe was entirely
random, then what had led Isaac to choose that
particular store out of all the shops and trading
posts in Gallup?

I didn't have the answer to that question...but I
also knew better than to doubt whatever forces had
sent us there.

Without replying, I turned on the engine.

"Let's head over to the hotel," I said.

Chapter 9
Riddle of the Rocks

E ven though we were about twenty minutes early, our rooms at the Hampton Inn were ready and waiting for us. Once again, I found myself wishing Isaac and I could share a room, but I knew we just weren't there yet. Despite all the time we'd spent together, I still wasn't quite able to quantify our relationship; he'd been a better friend to me than most of the people I'd left behind in Southern California, and yet I knew there was more to our connection than simple friendship. Otherwise, he wouldn't have felt compelled to kiss me that first time, or on all the occasions which followed. Exactly what he was waiting for, I honestly didn't know. He'd told me he wanted to take things slowly, and I'd said that was fine, but still, we'd been seeing one another for more than a month, and generally by this point, matters would have progressed to their logical conclusion.

At least, I thought that was how these things were supposed to work. All my previous relationships had ended up in bed after the third or fourth date, and Isaac and I had blown past our fourth date weeks earlier. I had to wonder if he wanted to hold off until he was entirely mobile, was free of the crutches altogether. With how quickly he'd been progressing over the last month, that day didn't seem as far off as it might once have. Still, it remained in a hazy, uncertain future, and I didn't think I wanted to wait that long.

If I were a little braver, I would have simply broached the subject with him and gotten it over with. But I wasn't. I'd rather have the status quo stay in place indefinitely than scare him off by trying to push him to move faster than he wanted to.

So, I dropped off my two bags in my room, and Isaac took his duffle into the hotel room two doors down from mine, and a few minutes later, we reconvened in the hallway.

"It looks like there's a fairly large campground at the state park," he said as he tucked his phone into his jacket pocket, making me think he'd been doing a little investigating while I was offloading my stuff. "Maybe we should park there first and get our bearings, and then decide what to do next."

Even though he hadn't said it out loud—probably because we were standing in a fairly public space—I guessed what he really meant was that we'd pause at the campground to see if the compass had decided to get its butt in gear and start working again, or whether I might have a flash of inspiration now that I was closer to the place where Mina Powers had died and had presumably hidden the patriarch's tears.

I had my doubts whether either of those things was going to happen, but I knew we needed to give it a try. "Sounds like a plan," I said, and we both headed down the hall to the elevator.

As we walked out into the parking lot, I couldn't help sliding a sideways glance toward Isaac's crutches. He hadn't said anything about them, hadn't told me whether he planned to wait in the car the way he had when I'd made the trek into the mountains outside Cimarron, or whether he'd been husbanding his strength so he could accompany me on this particular hike. Honestly, I didn't know for sure if he was really up to that kind of exertion. It didn't seem as if the long car ride had taken a toll on him the way our drive down from Taos and its environs had, but even so, it was a big jump from weathering a trip on my SUV's nicely padded seats to hiking around in the wilderness outside Gallup.

Well, I wouldn't say anything. Isaac knew

better than anyone else what he could or couldn't manage. And while I would have liked to have a companion along on this expedition, I also didn't want him to do anything that might jeopardize his health or the amazing progress he'd made so far.

It took about fifteen minutes to drive from the hotel to the state park. When we got there, I was a little startled by how downright civilized it seemed. I'd been expecting something like the rough campground outside Taos where that rocky outcropping had split apart and revealed the key to the hidden chamber on the eastern slopes of the Sangre de Cristo mountains, but this place had rows and rows of orderly campsites with power hookups, along with what looked like a meeting center of some sort and even a gift shop and what appeared to be a large ring for rodeos, complete with rows of stalls.

This was the place where a demon had hunted Mina to her death?

My expression must have turned dubious, because Isaac said, "It's not all like this. There are trails that wind for miles around in these hills, and parts of the park are pretty remote. You didn't see anything like this campground in your vision, did you?"

"Nope," I said flatly. "Nothing at all like this. I'm sure what we're looking for has to be hidden out on one of those trails."

One good thing about how downright civilized this part of the park had turned out to be—I was able to maneuver the Palisade into one of the parking spaces near the convention center and turn off the engine so we could get our bearings.

Back at the hotel, Isaac had downloaded a map of the park onto his phone, and he opened it now. "It looks like there are two main trails," he said, shifting the phone toward me so I could see the display on the screen. "Pyramid Rock and Church Rock. I was going to say we should try the Pyramid Rock one, since we're closer to the trailhead." He paused there, dark eyes speculative. "Unless you're getting some kind of vibe that tells you we should go to the other one."

Unfortunately, it seemed as though my witchy instincts—if I really had any at all—had decided to take a powder for the time being, since I wasn't feeling a damn thing.

Still, I had one other stratagem I could try.

I pulled the compass out of my pocket, but the needle only continued making its slow progress around the dial, just as it had for the past few hours. "Well, so much for that," I said, knowing how cranky I sounded. Even though we'd had a great lunch and an unexpectedly informative chat with the owner of the trading post, I still felt irritated, antsy. I didn't want to go wandering around in the wilderness. No, what I wanted to do was find an interesting local bar and have a margarita or something.

However, since blended drinks weren't in my immediate future, I knew I needed to suck it up and get with the program.

Being Isaac, he didn't give me the side-eye for sounding like a spoiled brat. No, he just said calmly, "Well, then, Pyramid Rock it is. The signs should show us which way to go."

I had to say that much for the park—everything was extremely well-marked, and so it was easy enough to follow the directions that led us past the rodeo arena and the horse stalls, and then bump along a dirt road to the trailhead itself. To be fair, even though the way wasn't paved, it clearly got graded at regular intervals, since the going was smoother than I'd expected it would be.

And then we got to the trailhead itself, which had space for about twenty or so cars to park. At that hour of the day and at that season, only two other vehicles occupied those spaces, a dusty black Xterra with a roof rack and one of those plastic water containers strapped to the rear door, and a shiny Jeep Wrangler that looked as though it had just been driven off the showroom floor.

I pulled the Palisade into an empty spot a bit away from the other two vehicles, then turned off the engine. The sun was definitely getting lower in the western sky, but I thought we still had a couple of hours of daylight left.

Isaac spoke before I could ask the awkward question. "I'll come with you part of the way."

I sent him a sideways glance. "Are you sure?"

His lips lifted in one of those quietly amused smiles I loved so much. "Don't worry—I'll stop as soon as I don't think I can go any further. How's your cell signal?"

A pause while I dug my new iPhone out of my purse. Part of the reason why I'd gone with Verizon rather than sticking with T-Mobile for my new phone was that I'd heard Verizon tended to do better in far-flung places, and there were a lot of those in New Mexico. Sure enough, I had two bars, plenty to get out a call or a text message, or even pull up a map on my phone if need be.

"Good enough," I said. "Yours?"

He swiveled his phone so I could see that it also had two bars—no big surprise, since his carrier was Verizon, too.

"It looks like we're set," he said. "Let's go and take a look around."

Because I knew he could maneuver in and out of the car with his crutches just fine, I went ahead and got out, and waited down by the rear of the SUV while he got himself situated and then took a few paces to stand by my side. We both glanced up the trail, and I frowned. The map had described both trails as "moderate," but I wasn't so sure about that. The going was rougher than I'd expected, and climbed steeply as it moved away from the trailhead. I had to admit I was anything but an experienced hiker, so maybe it looked more daunting to me than it actually was.

However, I didn't ask Isaac whether he was really sure about this. The last thing I wanted was to come off as some kind of hovering helicopter girlfriend or something.

If I was even his girlfriend at all. We'd never really sat down and tried to figure out the exact parameters of our relationship, and I wasn't about to start now.

"I think I can go the first hundred yards or so," he said quietly. "I'll let you know when I need to take a pause and assess."

That still sounded like an awful lot of hiking to me, but I had to believe he knew what he was doing.

"Okay," I said, and got the compass out of my pocket once again. Just like before, it didn't seem inclined to do a damn thing, but at least this way, it would be accessible in case it decided to wake up and be useful once more.

We began making our way up the trail—slowly, because Isaac's crutches wouldn't exactly allow him to take huge strides. That was fine by me, though; I didn't think it would be a good idea to exhaust myself on this lower part of the trail and then have nothing left in case I had to keep going without Isaac by my side.

The wind was cold, and so I was glad of the scarf I'd knotted around my neck and the puffer jacket I'd put on. The leather jacket that was my usual outerwear certainly wasn't up to northern New Mexico in November, and the gorgeous teal wool coat I'd bought in Albuquerque also wasn't appropriate to the occasion. Luckily, though, I'd picked up the puffer jacket a few weeks ago, figuring it would be a good choice for the times when wandering around in a wool coat simply wasn't feasible.

Isaac wore a similar style of jacket, although he hadn't bothered to cover his throat. Most likely, this sharp wind felt positively balmy to someone who'd been born and raised in Santa Fe. Would I ever get used to the cold, or would I spend my winters here feeling as though I was going to freeze my ass off every time I went outside?

Good question. For the moment, though, it seemed better to focus on my surroundings rather than brood about an indeterminate future that might or might not ever come to pass.

"Feel anything yet?" he asked.

"Besides thinking I'm going to freeze my ass off if I stay out here much longer?" I returned.

He grinned, teeth flashing in the afternoon

sun. "Well, I hope that won't happen," he said. "I kind of like your ass where it is."

About all I could do was shake my head, even as a flush that had nothing to do with the wind touched my cheeks at the good-humored compliment. "Anyway," I said, "no, I'm not feeling much. No weird vibes, no little tingles. Nothing to tell me this is anything more than a regular mountain trail that thousands of people walk on every year."

Oddly, Isaac didn't seem too discouraged by my remark. "Well, your visions told you that it happened in a remote spot. So, I'm not that surprised you aren't sensing anything this far down on the trail."

Good to know he was so Zen about the situation, even though I told myself he had a point. For all I knew, the canyon where Mina Powers had died wasn't connected to this trail at all. She could have used the Pyramid Rock trail as a starting point and then struck off across open land. There were signs posted everywhere telling people to remain on the marked path, but I could see how getting written up by a park ranger would be the least of someone's worries if they were being chased by demons.

About all I could do was lift my shoulders and keep going. Not too fast, although so far, it looked as though Isaac was managing the trail just fine— he didn't seem overly out of breath, and his face didn't have that pinched, tired look it got when he pushed himself past the limits of his endurance.

Which was good, but still, I had to believe he couldn't keep this up indefinitely.

We walked along in silence for the next few minutes. I could tell that Isaac wanted to refrain from being too chatty because he probably didn't want to distract me from feeling any vibes or getting any psychic flashes from the surrounding landscape...and most likely wanted to save his energy as well.

Problem was, I couldn't feel a damn thing. Well, except cold and increasingly tired, and wanting more and more to get out of this wind and back someplace where I could order a drink and maybe a nosh, like a plate of fries or some nachos.

"Okay," he said after a bit more time had passed, and then stopped, now leaning heavily on his crutches. "I don't think I can go any farther without risking my return trip to the car."

Right—the hike down would be easier, but it would still require enough energy that he couldn't completely wipe himself out now.

I paused and put my hands on my hips, gazing at the trail as it rose between rusty-hued rock outcroppings. Our surroundings were actually quite beautiful, but I hadn't been focusing on the scenery.

"I don't know whether I want to go any farther, either," I said.

His brows pulled together. "You hiked much farther than this when you went up to the cave to retrieve the sword."

Which was true, but....

"That was different," I argued. "I had the compass guiding me that time. Right now, I just feel like I'm wandering around in the wilderness without any clear direction."

"Like Moses," Isaac said, his mouth quirking a little.

Since I wasn't in any mood for a joke, I didn't bother to return the smile. "Well, I hope it won't take forty years, but yeah. Anyway, I don't think we're succeeding at anything here except tiring us both out."

He was silent for a moment as he glanced up at the trail ahead, and then let his gaze track to the east, where presumably the Church Rock trail lay. Then he said, "I think you may be right. Let's call it a day, and we can try the other trail tomorrow."

I wasn't feeling particularly sanguine about that one, either, since it was still close enough that I should have picked up some sort of vibes from it. Or the compass should have gotten its act together and started guiding us where we needed to go.

But I didn't bother to mention either of those worries. It was entirely possible that tomorrow would be a new day, and we'd find exactly what we were looking for.

Or we'd completely misinterpreted the clues of the riddle and were wandering around far, far away from the spot where Mina Powers had died, and where she'd supposedly hidden the patriarch's tears.

Whatever those were.

Even if we'd completely blundered here, I knew Isaac was right. We needed to quit while we were ahead, go back to the hotel, and try again tomorrow.

"Let's get going," I said. "And then we can check Yelp again and find out where to go for dinner...someplace where we can get a bottle of wine."

Now he grinned, dark eyes crinkling behind the sunglasses he wore. "It's a deal."

We actually were able to locate Gallup's equivalent of fine dining, a fun restaurant in a historic hotel, where they brought us a very nice bottle of local wine from a vintner in a place called Velarde, and where we had some steaks that seemed just as good as anything we could've gotten in Santa Fe.

On that Thursday night, the place wasn't too busy, but just busy enough that we both knew it wouldn't be safe to discuss our real reasons for being in town. However, talking about Red Rock State Park certainly wouldn't raise the eyebrows of anyone listening in, even if we couldn't bring up the supernatural reasons for wanting to explore it more fully.

And I also couldn't help saying, "It was pretty impressive what you did up on the trail today. I thought it was a pretty steep climb, and I wasn't even on crutches."

Maybe Isaac's shoulders lifted a little as he reached for his glass of wine. "Oh, it wasn't so bad. In a way, having the crutches might have helped, since they gave me a little extra stability—you know, like using a walking stick or hiking poles."

I hadn't really thought of it that way, but I supposed he had a point. Still, I doubted that most people who used hiking poles did so after surviving a car crash that should have killed them. "Maybe," I allowed before adding, "Is the Church Rock trail just as steep?"

Isaac shook his head. "It doesn't look like it. Both trails may be rated as 'moderate,' but the Pyramid Rock one gains a lot more elevation and is a bit longer. So, I may be able to go all the way to the end on Church Rock."

That comment sounded as though he was being a bit too ambitious about our prospects for the next day's hike. Then again, we'd be attempting the second trail when we were fresh, not near the end of the day after a long drive. About all I could do was hope we'd find some kind of clue or marker long before we made the entire hike, even if the chances of that happening didn't look very good at the moment.

"Here's hoping," I said, and decided I'd leave it there.

He seemed to get the message, because he didn't try to protest that of course he was up to that kind of physical activity. For all I knew, he was planning to cast another healing spell in the morning, or maybe even the enchantment that allowed him to walk unaided without his crutches. I wasn't sure that was the wisest plan of action, just because I didn't like the idea of him using up some of his magical energy before we even knew exactly what we might be facing on the trail. The last time he cast that spell, he'd ended up in his wheelchair for several days afterward, and we couldn't afford for him to be out of commission like that.

Instead, he surprised me by saying, "I know it's a few weeks off, but I was hoping you'd come to my brother Richard's house for Thanksgiving. We always have the gathering there—he's the oldest of us three, and so he seems to think it's his responsibility to take on the hosting duties. It can be a little chaotic with all the kids, but I think you'll have fun."

For a second or two, I just gazed back at Isaac, slightly gobsmacked. Oh, sure, he'd already mentioned once before that he'd like to spend time with me around the holiday, but because he hadn't brought up the subject since then, I wasn't sure whether he'd decided to quietly shelve the plan.

I should have known he would never do that to me.

"I'd love to," I said, hoping he hadn't taken my astonished silence the wrong way. "If your brother doesn't mind, of course."

Isaac's dark eyes twinkled a bit. "Actually, he's the one who just poked me about it—I got a text from him while I was getting changed for dinner. With all that's been going on, Thanksgiving sort of slipped my mind. But of course I want you to come and meet the family."

Meet the family. It sounded so formal. Yes, Isaac had already met my father, and they'd gotten along really well, but somehow, the thought of going to Isaac's brother Richard's house and being a guest on an occasion as important as Thanksgiving told me that he took our relationship seriously, that I wasn't some flash in the pan.

Which was pretty much exactly what I'd been hoping for, wasn't it? We might have only been together for a little more than a month, but I already knew I didn't want to visualize a future that didn't have Isaac Zamora in it.

"And I want to meet them," I said firmly. "You'll need to ask Richard if there's anything he'd like me to bring."

"Richard and Anita—she's his wife—wouldn't think of asking a guest to bring anything other than themselves." Isaac paused there, and once again that amused glint entered his dark eyes. "However, I don't think they'd be too offended if you brought over a bottle of wine."

"I think I can manage that," I said with a smile.

"Something to look forward to," he replied, and lifted his glass.

I touched mine to his, then swallowed some cabernet to seal the deal.

Now all we had to do was survive the next day.

Chapter 10
Going to Church

Isaac and I fortified ourselves with some enormous breakfast burritos the next morning before heading out. The hotel had thoughtfully supplied bottled water in our rooms, and we carried that with us, although I found myself wondering whether a single bottle of water would really be enough to keep each of us going through the entire hike. According to the trail maps he'd pulled up on his phone, the Church Rock trail was only a little over two miles from end to end, which really shouldn't be that big a deal.

Assuming we even stuck to the trail. The vision I'd had of Mina Powers running through that red rock canyon hadn't shown anything which looked like a true path, just open areas between clumps of rabbitbrush—called "chamisa" around here—and manzanita and dry grass. I was worried she'd ventured far from any areas that might be regularly trodden by hikers and tourists, and so we might be out in the wilderness for some time.

Well, at least it was a cool day in November, and not August or something. The skies weren't quite as clear today as they'd been the day before, but I told myself the little bit of cloud cover would probably help to moderate temperatures. The winds had died down a bit, too, and that would also help.

We followed the signs and parked in the dirt lot at the foot of the Church Rock trailhead. Since it was now Friday, there were more vehicles there than I'd seen in the Pyramid Rock parking lot the day before, although the place wasn't anywhere near full.

The two of us climbed out of the Palisade, and Isaac retrieved his crutches. He didn't seem to be leaning on them very much, though, telling me that right now, he was using them more because he knew he'd probably need them after walking the trail for a bit than because he couldn't manage on his own for the moment.

He sent me a questioning glance, and I shook my head. "Not a damn thing," I told him. "But we're not on the trail yet. Maybe once we get closer, I'll start to pick up some vibes."

"And the compass?"

More and more, I was beginning to think the enchanted compass wasn't going to help us at all, that it had shot its wad after guiding me to find the sword and was now nothing more than a pretty prop. However, I didn't argue, only dug the thing out of my coat pocket and flipped open the lid.

As far as I could tell, nothing about it had changed a single bit. The needle kept moving slowly around the dial, and it didn't look as though it intended to do anything else for the foreseeable future.

"Well, at least the paths are pretty clearly marked, so it's not as if we really need it," Isaac remarked, and I slanted him a wry look.

"They're well marked here," I returned. "Who knows what they're going to be like farther up the trail?"

He didn't seem too put out by my response, and only lifted his shoulders. "I guess we'll just have to wait and see."

I shook my head and returned the compass to my pocket. "I guess so."

There wasn't much left to do after that convo than begin to make our way along the trail, a dusty ochre path cutting through banks of chamisa and dry grass, along with a scrubby juniper tree here and there to provide a bit of contrast. As Isaac had told me the day before, this way seemed a lot easier than the Pyramid Rock trail, although I didn't know for sure whether that was actually a good thing or not. If Mina Powers really had come this way while trying to elude the demon who was out for her blood, wouldn't she have gone someplace with rougher terrain, a spot where she might have a better chance of shaking off her pursuer?

As with so many other aspects of this mystery, it was impossible for me to say. The woman who'd provided the egg that helped to conceive me was still a cipher in so many ways, despite the glimpses I'd gotten of her.

I had a feeling I'd never completely figure out what had motivated her to sell her eggs, even though I guessed there was a lot more going on here than a simple need to raise some cash.

In the meantime, though, I needed to buckle down and do my best to find the patriarch's tears.

A glance over at Isaac told me he seemed to be chugging along just fine, and didn't appear to be winded or flagging in any way, although of course we were walking more slowly than I would have if I'd been going it alone. But that was fine; we weren't on a set schedule here, so this little expedition could take as long as it needed.

After we'd gone about a quarter mile or so, another man and woman, probably in their early forties, caught up with Isaac and me and then kept going after giving the two of us a quick smile. However, I thought I saw the slightest hint of puzzlement on the face of the woman, as though she couldn't quite figure out why someone on crutches would even be attempting such a hike.

Well, let her think what she wanted. It wasn't as though people with physical challenges didn't compete in paralympics and participate in all kinds of outdoor activities, so I didn't think a guy on crutches walking along a trail that was only moderately difficult should be that big a deal.

Also, because the path had been marked with little rock cairns every twenty feet or so, it was almost impossible to lose our way. If we'd simply come here to get off the beaten path and spend some time in the great outdoors, I would have been enjoying myself.

As it was, I couldn't quite get rid of the knot of tension at the back of my neck, the one that told me I should be feeling some sort of twinge, some kind of sensation that would let me know I was on the right path and not just wandering around in the wilderness because I was too stupid to correctly interpret the clues Mina Powers had left behind.

Doing my best to push aside my disquiet, I glanced over at Isaac and said, "Still hanging in there?"

He gave a short nod, as though he didn't want to expend any more effort than was strictly necessary. "So far, so good. I'm not sure why they rated this trail as moderate, since it seems so much easier than the Pyramid Rock one."

I was inclined to agree. Or rather, I was feeling pretty good about the situation...until we came around a curve, and the trail ended.

All right, it didn't end, end. But the only way to proceed from here was to climb a set of stairs cut into the rocks themselves, a feat Isaac would never be able to manage on his crutches.

"Well, I guess that's that," he said, staring up at the steeply pitched rock staircase.

He sounded matter-of-fact, not annoyed or frustrated the way I probably would have. "So, what do we do?" I asked.

"You go on from here, and I wait," he replied. "I don't think we should turn back, but it's pretty obvious that I can't climb those stairs." A pause as he pulled his cell phone out of his jacket pocket. "I've only got one bar, but it should be enough to get a text message through. You?"

I also got out my phone and took a quick glance down at the screen. "Same here."

"Then at least we shouldn't have to worry about being out of contact." He stopped there, then came a little closer and left one crutch propped under his arm so he could reach over and give me a reassuring pat on the shoulder. "You'll do fine. You had to get the sword on your own, after all."

Yes, I did. But something about this situation felt different, even though I couldn't say exactly why.

Scratch that—I knew why. Back then, I'd had the compass guiding me, and so I'd known I was heading in the right direction, even if I hadn't known what I was looking for. This time, I'd be going in blind, trusting that something would tell me at some point where I was supposed to be heading.

Also, even though we had cell service here, that didn't mean my one feeble bar would continue to hang on as I progressed farther along the trail. If it dropped out completely, what was I supposed to do then?

Keep going, I scolded myself. *It's a hiking trail, not the jungles of Borneo. People come along here on a daily basis. It's not like you're going to be in the middle of absolutely nowhere.*

True enough, but accidents happened all the time, even on well-trodden hiking paths.

But we'd come all this way, and turning back now wasn't really an option, not if I wanted to solve the riddle and find the patriarch's tears. Something was telling me they were just as important as the sword I'd found a few weeks earlier, even if I didn't know exactly why.

"Sure," I said easily, although I guessed my blithe tone didn't fool Isaac for a minute, not after I'd hesitated so long in replying. "I'll text you if I find anything."

"Sounds good," he said, then leaned down to give me an unexpected but very welcome kiss. "Be careful."

I didn't tell him I was always careful, because I'd be the first person to admit that sometimes I jumped the gun and leaped into things before I'd weighed all the pros and cons. But since I was out of my element here, I knew I'd proceed with as much caution as possible.

"I will," I promised, then made myself turn away from him and start climbing the rock stairs.

They looked more intimidating than they actually were, smoothed by years of use and thousands of feet, climbing at a sharper angle than regular household stairs, but not steep enough that I couldn't manage as long as I took it slowly and didn't try to look back. However, it was clear to me that Isaac couldn't have managed the rock staircase, not without laboriously hauling himself up to each step and pausing to get his bearings before he moved on to the next one, an exertion that would have exhausted him in only a couple of minutes.

That still didn't mean I was thrilled about leaving him behind.

I made it up the stairs and on to a more level

portion of the trail, although it continued to slope upward, heading toward the pinnacle of rock at the summit that I guessed gave the trail its name, since the formation did look a little bit like a church spire. And good thing it was so visible, because otherwise, I had a feeling I would have lost my way several times despite the cairns that marked the trails and the helpful ribbons people had left hanging from some of the trees.

Just as I was getting close to another of those rock stairs, I had such a sharp, sudden pain in the side of my neck that for a second, I thought I must have been stung by a bee or maybe a wasp, even though I'd seen very few insects on the hike so far. I put a hand to my neck, thinking I would feel the beginnings of a welt, but my skin felt smooth enough beneath my fingertips.

And then I realized why I'd felt that awful twinge. A path—barely a clear foot or two between clumps of rabbitbrush—wound away from the main trail, leading down into a canyon.

A red rock canyon.

No, from where I stood, I didn't recognize the place at all, and yet I somehow knew if I scrambled down the side of the hill and made my way along the canyon floor, it would begin to feel uncomfortably familiar.

That was where I needed to go.

I paused and got out my phone, and checked

the bars. Or rather, where the bars were supposed to be. Instead, I had that lovely "no service" message displayed in the upper left-hand corner of the screen.

So much for that idea.

No point in crying over no cell service, though. I got the bottle of water out of my backpack-style purse, allowed myself a couple of swallows, and then screwed down the cap and returned the bottle to my pack.

One more thing I needed to check, though.

Oh, yeah, the compass had definitely decided to wake up now. Instead of continuing with its lazy circuit of the dial, the needle had swung to the northeast, indicating the same direction as that wonderful twinge in my neck. That seemed to clinch the matter.

Time to get moving.

Once again, I found myself wishing I'd gotten my act together and bought some real hiking boots before we left on this expedition. In fact, I made a mental vow to myself that if I survived this scramble down the hillside, I'd go to the REI in Santa Fe as soon as I got back to town and make sure I was properly outfitted in case I had to do even more exploring to find the remaining answers to the riddle. After all, even if I did manage to locate the patriarch's tears, there was that whole "circle of iron" thing to figure out.

Well, sufficient to the day and all that. I'd worry about the iron circle after I had the patriarch's tears safely in hand.

My work boots slipped here and there, but somehow I managed to make it all the way down the path without landing on my ass or falling over a cliff or anything. The floor of the canyon was rough as well, strewn with enough rocks and boulders to tell me water definitely must flow through here during monsoon season, although things were dry enough at the moment, thank God.

The compass still pointed northeast, and so I followed it along the canyon floor, the skin at the back of my neck beginning to prickle as my surroundings grew more familiar—that sheer red rock wall to one side, the smoother shape of a mountain off to the left.

This was definitely the canyon from my vision, the one that had blindsided me when I put on Mina's eyeglasses for the first time.

I stopped and looked in all directions, but I was utterly alone here, without even the call of a bird or the hum of an insect to break the silence. The only sound was the wind in the dry grasses.

My utter solitude should have been reassuring —at least it didn't look as though anyone had come through here recently, and I definitely didn't have any demons on my tail—and yet an uneasy chill worked its way down my back, a shiver that didn't have much to do with the wind that had just picked up, pulling a few strands of hair loose from the messy twist I'd used to contain it earlier that morning.

It's just because you saw this place in a vision and know what happened here, I told myself, but that didn't help as much as I'd thought it would. Knowing that Mina Powers had died somewhere in this lonely canyon was just too unsettling.

Well, I was here now. The only thing I could do was keep going and see how all this played out.

The canyon grew narrower as I headed east, and my surroundings began to feel unfamiliar again. For a minute or two, I couldn't quite figure that out, and then I realized Mina had been running *from* this place, not to it.

Trying to get away before the demon who was pursuing her could find out what she'd really been up to?

A few more minutes of walking seemed to prove that theory, because I could now tell the canyon was of the box variety as the walls narrowed and the entire thing came to an abrupt end, the sandstone walls partially obscured by some surprisingly lush pine trees and a few bare-limbed varieties that I thought might be oak.

The Penny Briggs of a few weeks ago might have been stumped by this development, but I now knew that a bare rock wall could be a lot more than it seemed. I pulled out the compass and saw it still pointed northeast, right at the terminus of the canyon.

I waited a moment, wondering if there was going to be an earth tremor like the one that had split the one outcropping apart and vomited up the box that held the key to the sword chamber, but nothing happened.

Clearly, I was supposed to get in some other way.

That key had traveled with me as well, threaded onto my key ring along with the much more prosaic ones to my rented house. I pulled the keys out of my pack and sort of brandished the magic key, hoping that might do the trick.

The rock didn't budge, and I let out an exasperated breath.

Couldn't Mina Powers have made this just a little bit easier?

Probably not, or the demons might have found the treasures she'd worked so hard to conceal.

Too bad I'd never been someone who played *World of Warcraft* or any other video games—or even *Dungeons and Dragons*—or maybe I would have known right away what to do to get inside the mountain. But since no one was watching, I supposed it didn't matter if I made an utter fool of myself.

I took the key and laid it against the rock,

hoping maybe physical contact would work when mere proximity hadn't. No door yawned within the rock wall, and no earthquake came to shake some boulders loose and reveal a hidden passageway.

Scowling, I returned the key ring to my pack, then took a step back and set my hands on my hips as I glared at the blank surface. Surely this was where I was meant to be, or the compass wouldn't have guided me here. However, having done its work, it seemed content to sit back and wait for me to figure out what to do next.

Okay, fine.

"Mina," I said. "It's your daughter, Penny. You've left something here for me, but I don't know how to get it. Want to help a girl out?"

And then I waited.

Once again, not a damn thing happened.

This was getting ridiculous.

Feeling desperate, I went up to the rock and placed both hands flat against it, hoping that maybe it needed physical contact with someone who shared Mina's DNA. The stone was cold against my bare skin, faintly rough, but I didn't feel anything more than that.

What the hell was I missing?

I lifted my hands from the rock wall and rubbed them against my thighs, getting off the bit of dust and grime I'd attracted by laying them flat against the stone. For a long moment, I stood there, feeling ridiculous even though there was no one around to witness my failure.

Oddly, an image from *The Lord of the Rings* came swimming up in my memory, the scene where the Fellowship was trying to gain entry to the Mines of Moria. Not the sort of place you really wanted to go wandering around in, as it turned out, but the thing that stuck out in my mind was how they'd had to say a special word to get the hidden doors of the mine to open and let them in.

Was my bio-mom a *Lord of the Rings* fan?

What was the word Gandalf had said, anyway? Something Elvish, if I recalled correctly.

But then I had a flash of insight. Mina Powers hadn't expected me to quote Gandalf's lines. No, she'd left me her own charm for opening the box canyon's hidden door.

I gathered a breath, then said,

"*Ride the roan to find the patriarch's tears.*
Pour out a blessing to bury one's fears.
As above, so below,
Circle of iron to cast down your foe."

A low, groaning sound filled my ears, one that felt as though it had emanated from the very center of the earth.

Then a small, rounded door, nearly hidden by the juniper trees that clustered nearby, slowly opened, revealing a dark doorway that reminded me of nothing more than an open mouth. Once again, cold shivered its way down my spine, but I did my best to ignore it.

I'd come this far.

Time to go in.

Chapter 11
Tears of a Clown

Even if I'd skimped on the hiking boots, I'd at least had the foresight to throw a small but powerful Maglite into my bag, and so I didn't have to risk running down the battery on my phone to see where I was going. Unlike the chamber where I'd found the sword, there was no unearthly glow here, nothing to show that I was going in the right direction.

Well, except the compass, which pointed straight down the dark corridor where I now found myself.

It was low, too, just cramped enough that I had to bend my head slightly as I moved forward or risk giving myself a nasty knock on the head. I didn't know whether I was truly going to find the patriarch's tears in here, but I could tell I was going to end up with a nasty crick in my neck by the time I was done.

The rock hallway's floor was rougher, too, uneven enough that I tripped once and almost bashed myself in the forehead against the ceiling as I tried to regain my balance.

Maybe Mina had been in more of a hurry when she created this corridor. That made some sense, considering her demon pursuer had obviously been hot on her heels at the time.

Moving more slowly—and flashing the Maglite all around to make sure there weren't any other hazards lying in wait—I continued along the hall-way, noticing as I went that it sloped downward, as though drawing me deep into the bowels of the mountain.

Somehow, that wasn't a very comforting thought.

But, as I'd already told myself, I'd come this far, and I wasn't about to turn around now.

Well, unless there were rabid bats...giant poiso-nous   millipedes...not-quite-hibernating rattlesnakes.

I told my brain to shut up, and grasped the Maglite more firmly. So far, I hadn't seen any evidence of bugs or snakes or bats or anything else in here. No, it was only a simple stone corridor, almost a tunnel, and nothing more.

However, as I continued to walk and didn't see

any evidence of the hallway ending any time soon, I had to wonder just how deep into the mountain I was going. Was it really possible that Mina Powers could have dug all this herself?

The answer to that question revealed itself soon enough, as the stone corridor ended and I emerged into a larger space that looked as though it must have once been part of a mine, judging by the rough timbers that crossed the ceiling and supported sections of the walls. My best guess was that she'd utilized one of the former shafts to access her hiding place, with the only real magic being the door she'd concealed within the rock wall.

In fact, the illumination from the Maglite showed me a pair of intact rails from the mining operation, and an ore cart sitting on them.

Oh, no way. She wasn't seriously expecting me to get all *Temple of Doom* in here, was she?

Apparently so, because the cart shifted slightly when the beam from the Maglite moved across it, as though inviting me to climb inside. Another enchantment, obviously, but….

I really, really didn't want to get in that cart. What if there were murderous Kali worshippers hiding somewhere deep within the mine?

Okay, the rational side of my brain told me that was just stupid. I somehow doubted Mina would have sent me all this way, only to have to dodge a bunch of human-sacrificing priests as I got closer to my goal. No, she'd simply found a place that had the infrastructure she needed, and had set her own enchantments on top of it to make the mine serve her needs.

So get in the damn cart, Penny.

Before I could lose my nerve, I closed up the few paces between me and the ore cart, and climbed inside. Almost before I'd seated myself on the dusty floor, the thing began moving, reminding me a little too much of the Indiana Jones ride at Disneyland.

More magic, or merely my weight causing it to shift from its current position so gravity could pull it downward?

And it really didn't help that it was so dark in here, that I felt more as though I was inside Space Mountain, or maybe the gloomiest section of the Haunted Mansion ride rather than Disney's Temple of Doom ride. I gripped the side of the cart with my free hand, hoping it wouldn't speed up so much that I'd get tossed right out of my precarious seat and into the Stygian depths on either side.

Because I definitely was moving down. I did my best to keep the Maglite pointed forward so I could see where I was going, but since the ride in the ore cart wasn't exactly as smooth as it would have been in my Hyundai Palisade, the flashlight's beam bobbed and danced, making it almost impossible to get a good read on my surroundings. I could tell I was in another tunnel, this one larger than the one I'd traversed to get to the spot where the cart had been waiting for me, but otherwise, I wasn't able to make out very much.

No, I could only cling grimly to the cart, all the while wondering where I was going to end up, and how the hell I was supposed to get out of here even if I did make it to my destination more or less unscathed. Logic told me there had to be a tunnel somewhere that led back up to the ore cart chamber, one that would have been used by miners on foot, but right then, I could well imagine being entombed in here forever, lost in unmarked passageways until I turned into nothing more than a skeleton that would serve as a warning to future travelers not to wander in these treacherous mines.

Don't be ridiculous, I scolded myself. *If you're not back in a few hours, Isaac will send out some park rangers to look for you.*

Maybe so, but would they be able to track me to the red rock canyon, let alone into the mine itself? The doorway I'd used was magic, and wouldn't simply appear just because a bunch of ordinary mortals came wandering nearby.

And there has to be a real entrance somewhere, I thought. *Mina made the doorway for you...maybe... but it's not like the miners would have come and gone that same way.*

Again, logical enough. Even so, my entire body

was cold from fear, even though the air felt almost stuffy down here, and I probably didn't need to have my puffer coat zipped up quite so tightly. However, there wasn't much I could do at this point except hang on and hope my ride through the darkness would end sooner rather than later.

Which it actually did, the ore cart sliding to a slow stop in a large open space that seemed to be some kind of staging chamber for the carts, since there were roughly a half dozen of them queued up at the end of the track. In fact, my own cart bumped gently into one of them as I came to the end of my journey, telling me I would have to go from here on foot.

Exactly where I was supposed to go, I had no idea. But I knew I couldn't travel any farther while sitting in this cart, and so I climbed out, Maglite still clutched awkwardly in one hand, and then flashed it around so I could get my bearings.

This chamber looked like it must have been the confluence of many different tunnels, since I saw a bunch of them branching out from the spot where I stood, sort of like spokes on a wheel. With that many options to choose from, I really couldn't begin to guess which passageway hid the patriarch's tears—if they were down here at all. So far, nothing seemed particularly magical about this mine or the tunnels that snaked through it.

Well, except for the way I'd gotten in.

And while the relative mundanity of my surroundings should have reassured me, I couldn't quite keep myself from wondering if I really had made a colossal blunder and gone in exactly the wrong direction from where Mina had wanted me to go. Nothing I'd encountered so far seemed to have pointed me anywhere else, but if I really had been intended to end up down here in this Grand Central Station of mining tunnels, why wasn't I being given a sign as to where I should go next?

Grumbling a curse under my breath, I used my free hand to dig the compass out of my pocket and then shone the Maglite down at the dial. The dial was still spinning around and around, a little more quickly than before, as if it knew it needed to be doing something but was having a hard time getting its bearings.

Weren't we all.

Since there wasn't much else I could do, I stood there and waited. Eventually, the needle on the compass slowed, then came to a complete stop, pointing directly at a tunnel off to my left in roughly the south-southwest position.

Well, that looked like the sign I'd been waiting for.

I didn't return the compass to my pocket, but instead kept holding it in front of me as I shone the flashlight down the passage. From what I could tell, it looked like a typical mineshaft, with the rails for the ore cart gradually disappearing into blackness.

No bats or snakes or giant glowing slugs, which was a good thing.

Still holding the compass in one hand and the Maglite in the other, I began to make my way along the tunnel, my footsteps unnaturally loud as they sounded against the aged railroad ties. Part of me wanted to turn around and say the hell with all of this, but I told myself that if Mina Powers could manage to hide all this stuff in various locations around New Mexico while on the run from demons, then the least I could do was give her the courtesy of seeing this through to the end.

Because there wasn't really any way to mark the passage of the minutes—my phone was tucked safely in my pack, and I didn't have a free hand to dig it out—I couldn't tell how long I'd been walking, or how much distance I'd traveled. There was only the bobbing of the flashlight in the darkness, and the crunch of sand and rocks under my work boots for what felt like an interminable amount of time.

Eventually, though, the Maglite's beam wasn't just disappearing into the darkness, but shining against a rock wall with a wooden door built into it —a big door, large as something you'd find on a barn. What it was doing down here in the bottom of a mine, I had no idea. Possibly it had been used for storing equipment or unused ore carts.

I supposed I'd discover its purpose soon enough.

A large iron bar held it shut. I pocketed the compass and then used my free hand to lift the bar out of the way and swing the door outward.

Inside was utter blackness.

Great. I could have really done with some of the golden glow from the sword's hidden chamber right about now.

But the sword was safely stowed under the passenger seat of my Palisade. Maybe I should have brought it along, but Isaac's friend Santiago had only made a normal scabbard for it, not the sort of thing I could have strapped to my back, and I'd known that trying to hike around Church Rock with a sword in its sheath banging against my leg with every step probably wasn't a good idea. Also, I could only imagine the looks I would have gotten from other hikers on the trail if I'd been striding along next to them with a sword at my hip.

Well, the trusty Maglite had gotten me this far. I'd just have to hope it would allow me to see whatever I needed to find inside the chamber.

I pointed the flashlight's beam straight ahead and moved it from side to side, doing my best to illuminate as much of the space as possible. From what I could tell—since I wasn't exactly an expert on mining equipment—the chamber did appear to be pretty much what I'd thought it was, a place for storing ore carts and various bits and pieces of machinery that were either not being used or had fallen out of repair.

And I thought that stack of boxes off to one side might contain dynamite, although I couldn't know for sure unless I lifted one of the lids.

Considering how unstable the TNT must have been after all those years of sitting neglected underground, I didn't think poking at it was a very good idea.

But as I moved the flashlight's beam back to dead center, it caught a gleam of something metallic, something that looked almost golden. I had no idea what they'd once mined here, but I thought I remembered reading somewhere that most of the mines in New Mexico yielded silver and copper and turquoise and uranium, but not a lot of gold.

Whatever that object was, it didn't seem to me as though it was supposed to be here.

Moving cautiously, I stepped closer, making sure the beam remained trained on the gleaming item ahead of me. Once I was a few feet away, I realized it sat on a stack of crates, looking very out of place in that dark, dusty environment.

It was an orb, the sort of thing you might see in a painting of a medieval monarch. The gold caught by the flashlight's beam was a cross that cradled the glass within—or maybe the whole thing had been carved from rock crystal, since glass seemed too fragile to have lasted down here all these years.

Inside the glass…or crystal…was a clear liquid.

The patriarch's tears?

Maybe. I couldn't think what else that liquid might be. I kind of doubted something so valuable would be holding a bunch of ordinary tap water.

As I came closer, I saw that the band around its circumference, rather than being studded with precious jewels the way most of those things were, instead had writing engraved into the gold in elegant capital letters. Unfortunately, I couldn't read any of that writing, because I was pretty sure it was in Latin.

The cross at the top, though, was a gorgeous thing, studded with bezel-set sapphires and emeralds and pearls, with what I thought was a rough diamond in the center. Despite the dustiness of the surrounding chamber—and all the tunnels I'd just traveled through—the orb itself looked as though it had been recently polished, or that some magic quality about it had kept it from being touched by anything so plebeian as ordinary dirt.

Because I had to believe the thing was magical. Otherwise, why would Mina Powers have hidden it away so carefully in an abandoned mine?

Even though I had to believe she must have left it behind for me to find, I still hesitated to reach out and touch the orb. No, I wasn't quite as afraid of getting zapped as I might once have been, considering I'd retrieved the sword without suffering any magical attacks, but still. Something about this artifact felt different from the sword, even if I couldn't say exactly why.

But I hadn't come here just to take a few selfies with an orb. I needed to bring it back with me, even if I couldn't yet begin to guess at its purpose.

As beautiful as the object was, it was also small enough to ride out of here in my purse/backpack. It felt sort of sacrilegious to stick it in there with my phone and wallet and little travel pack of Kleenex, but I couldn't exactly carry the thing, not when I needed both hands to hold the compass and Maglite while navigating my way out of the mine.

When I lifted the orb, the gold and crystal felt icy cold against my hand...but only for a moment. Almost as soon as it came in contact with my flesh, it warmed quickly, and the liquid inside took on a faint glow.

Well, its reaction seemed like a sign from the universe that I was meant to find the thing.

The clear signal made me relax a little, although I realized the soft glow from the orb really wasn't sufficient to light my way out of here. No, I'd have to keep relying on the Maglite.

So, the orb went into my pack, and I slung it over one shoulder this time rather than having it lie flat against my back, mostly because it seemed less likely to get squished in that position. Another quick look around to make sure I hadn't missed anything, but the orb seemed to be the only thing here I'd been meant to find—there weren't any boxes on daises or golden compasses or any other artifacts of significance. Just a bunch of abandoned and broken-down equipment that had been left here because it wasn't worth hauling away.

I still didn't know what the circle of iron was, but it didn't look as though Mina had hidden it here.

To my relief, as soon as I left the oversized storage room, the compass's needle spun around again, pointing back the way I'd come. At least it didn't seem as though it meant to leave me down here once I'd located the object I'd been sent to find. I probably shouldn't have worried, because it had done exactly the same thing on my quest for the sword, leading me safely back out of the cave and down the trail to the dirt lot where Isaac was waiting for me.

All right, then. I made my way along that endless corridor, eventually returning to the spot where the mine cart I'd ridden down here sat on the tracks next to its companions. However, rather than springing to life the moment I appeared, it just sat there, its work apparently done.

Just as I was about to mutter a curse, though,

the compass came to my aid, pointing toward a tunnel I'd noticed previously but hadn't really inspected, since I'd been intent on following the compass's guidance. Now it pointed me in that direction, letting me know that was the best way to get out of here on foot.

Or at least, I hoped that's what it was telling me.

But since I didn't have any better options, I followed its lead, making my way along the passage. Like the first one I'd entered at the beginning of this little jaunt, it had a low ceiling, and so I had to bend my head to avoid bashing myself against the rocky surface. In a way, that was a good thing, because the tunnel slanted steeply, and bending forward as I climbed made it a little easier to maintain my balance.

This went on for a lot longer than I would have liked, especially since I knew now more than ever that I was going to have the mother of all cricks in my neck by the time I finally got out of this damn mine. But even though I was out of breath and probably should have paused to sip some water from the bottle in my pack, I kept at it doggedly, wanting to get out of this darkness so I could breathe some fresh air again.

Eventually, I glimpsed a spot of light ahead that I thought might be the outdoors, telling me I'd obviously come out a different way than the tunnel

I'd taken to get in here. That light seemed to shift and move, and as I got closer, I saw why—a large juniper tree obscured most of the opening, probably ensuring that it would be almost impossible to tell there was an opening to the mine here at all.

Despite the ache in my leg muscles, I speeded up my pace, wanting nothing more than to get out of there as quickly as possible. A cold breeze touched my face, reminding me of the brisk November day that waited for me.

And then I was outside, breathing in gulps of the crisp air, thrilled beyond belief to see the sun again, even if it was partially obscured by clouds. Because it was almost directly overhead, I realized I probably had been inside the mine for no more than an hour or two, nothing close to the horrible span of time I'd imagined while wandering down there in the dark.

I smiled as the sunlight touched my face. Now all I had to do was get down the hill and show Isaac what I'd found.

No need for the Maglite anymore. I shut it off and put it in my pocket, then consulted the compass. It pointed almost due west.

A quick glance around told me I'd emerged in a canyon not so different from the one where the hidden entrance to the mine was located—same red rock canyon walls, same scrubby junipers and dried-out chamisa. There was even a faint path threading its way through the dead grass and brush, a path I hoped would lead me back to the main trail.

Chin up, I began to make my way along the path...only to be stopped a few seconds later by a huge shape that appeared to boil up out of the ground itself, all glowing red eyes and black scales and a long, barb-edged tail.

"Going somewhere?" the demon asked.

Chapter 12
Pontifex Flex

Although I'd only started to learn how to use the thing, my hand still moved by reflex to my hip—a hip that was noticeably bare of swords at the moment, since the magical demon-killing blade I'd found a month earlier was still tucked under the passenger seat of my Palisade.

Well, shit.

I took a step backward, even though I doubted the little bit of extra distance was going to do me much good. "What do you want?" I asked, doing my best to sound tough and not at all concerned that seven feet plus of hulking supernatural muscle was blocking my way.

The demon's red eyes narrowed. "Oh, I think you know. That pretty bauble in your pack—give it to me."

Exactly how the demon had sensed that I'd

stowed the orb in my backpack, I had no idea. He shouldn't have even known I was here, since I still wore the protection amulet around my throat in addition to the turquoise necklace that had once belonged to Mina Powers. But somehow he'd realized I had the thing, and my stomach knotted with worry over what else he might know.

Still, since he hadn't made an immediate move to separate my head from my neck, I thought I should try stalling a bit. "I don't know what you're talking about," I told him.

His blood-red eyes narrowed. In appearance, this particular demon didn't look too different from the other two I'd encountered recently, except he was much taller and broader, and looked like he could probably snack on linebackers for breakfast. Also, his features seemed just slightly more refined, a little more human, although I didn't think he'd be gracing the cover of *GQ* any time soon.

"You know exactly what I'm talking about," he growled. "Hand it over."

Why was he asking at all, rather than just knocking me down and taking the orb? It wasn't as though I could possibly beat him in a physical confrontation.

But then his gaze shifted for just a fraction of a second, moving toward the pair of necklaces I wore before our eyes locked once more.

Was he afraid of the amulet? Maybe it couldn't quite shield my presence from the demon, but it was still enough to offer protection from a physical assault.

"Tell me why first," I said, and he blinked.

Clearly, he hadn't expected me to make that sort of a request. Judging by the mixture of annoyance and astonishment that passed over his quasi-human face, he'd been expecting me to cower before him and give him the orb without argument. "Why what?" he demanded, his tone rough as sandpaper.

"Why do you want it?"

Rather than reply directly, he said, "It doesn't belong to you."

I crossed my arms. "Does it belong to *you?*"

Now he looked almost confused, and I had to smother a grin. He reached up to scratch his head, which had the same mane of long black hair as the demon I'd killed a few weeks earlier, and then he scowled, engraving fierce lines between his heavy black brows.

"It will, after you give it to me."

Talk about a one-track mind. "I found it fair and square," I replied, matching him stare for stare. "And honestly, since it's been sitting at the bottom of a mine shaft for decades, I don't think anyone else is going to come along and claim it. I kind of doubt that something with a big old cross sitting on top of it is the sort of thing a demon uses to decorate his living room."

A corner of his lip lifted, revealing a sharp yellow fang. "You have no idea what you're talking about, mortal. I'm trying to be nice here. Hand it over, and you can walk away with your skin intact."

He took a single step toward me and paused. The thick muscles of his neck tensed, though, giving me the impression that it had taken a huge effort for him to close up the distance between us even that much. Another effect from the protection amulet I wore, or was he somehow reacting to the orb stowed inside my bag?

The words sounded in my mind, even though that inner voice didn't sound much like mine.

You don't have the sword, but you can use the orb. Use the tears.

Was that Mina Powers somehow speaking to me across unimaginable voids of time and space?

Possibly. Maybe one day I'd have the chance to sit down and figure all this out, but for now, I thought I'd better heed the advice that inner voice had given me.

"Okay, okay," I said, holding out a hand...as though that ineffectual gesture would be enough to keep the unholy creature from advancing another step in my direction. "Just give me a sec."

The demon paused. "No tricks."

"None," I lied blithely.

I slid the pack off my shoulder and rooted around inside. My fingers closed on the surface of the orb, now almost too hot to touch. Was it reacting to the presence of the demon?

Something else I'd have to puzzle out later. I took the orb from my bag, wondering even as I did so how in the hell I was supposed to get the liquid or tears or whatever they were out of there, since the thing seemed to be sealed up pretty tight.

But even as I began to extend my hand and the demon moved closer, his own hands reaching for the orb, a stream of water arced out from the rough diamond in the center of the cross and hit him right in the face.

At once, he let out an unearthly howl and began clawing at his skin, shredding the scales there, as though he hoped if he could remove the ones the liquid had touched, he might be able to prevent the watery substance from causing any further harm.

No such luck, though. The tears seemed to act like some kind of highly corrosive acid on his unearthly flesh, because as I looked on in horror, he continued to disintegrate until nothing was left except a nasty little puddle of black liquid in the middle of the path. The whole process had taken only a few seconds, and definitely hadn't given me enough time to try to intervene...even if I'd wanted to.

Some kind of holy water, I thought dazedly. Despite the weird mixture of horror and relief I was currently experiencing, I still remembered how Isaac had used that very thing to break down the corpse of the demon I'd killed in my house on Halloween.

Except this stuff had acted much, much faster, and had killed the demon outright, rather than merely disintegrating an already dead body. Whatever kind of holy water it was, it obviously had to be some pretty potent stuff.

No wonder the demon had wanted to make sure it stayed out of human hands.

With shaking fingers, I returned the orb to my pack and zipped it up tight. Once I was done, I glanced down at the ground, only to see that the black liquid the demon had left behind was now gone as well.

However, the path wasn't entirely empty. Lying where the demon's nasty remains had been only a moment earlier was a small bronze medallion. Although I really didn't want to touch the thing, I also didn't think it was a very good idea to leave it behind, either.

The metal was cool to the touch when I picked it up. One side was completely plain, but on the other, the bronze had been stamped with a complicated device or sigil of some kind, something that looked almost like the crenellations of a medieval castle along the top and a bunch of shapes that appeared to be Maltese crosses hanging from the bottom.

I didn't recognize the design—not that I'd expected to. My powers might have been waking up, but what I didn't know about the strange magical world I'd stumbled into could have fit onto an aircraft carrier.

I could only hope that Isaac might help me figure out what it was...and what it meant. First, though, I had to get back to the spot where he was waiting for me.

After shoving the medallion in my jeans pocket, I headed down the path and prayed I was going in the right direction. Just like the canyon I'd followed on my way in, this place didn't show any sign of people coming through here any time in recent memory. Yes, there was the path, but that could have been made by deer.

Or coyotes, or bears. I kept looking from side to side, but I didn't see any signs of life, not even the shadow of a hawk overhead.

Probably a good thing, considering the vultures I'd spied in one of my first visions from Mina's eyeglasses, a vision that had shown me a whole lot more than I wanted to see.

But I had my sort of trusty compass, and the needle still pointed straight ahead. I had to hope I was going in the right direction, and pray the compass hadn't decided to stop working for some reason.

My doubts were proved wrong in the next few minutes as the path began to slope upward and I saw how it kept climbing, moving in a direction that should lead me back to the Church Rock trail. It looked like a rough scramble, though, one where I'd probably need both hands.

With some reluctance, I slipped the compass into my pocket, hoping I wouldn't need any further guidance because I now mostly knew where I was supposed to go. As I'd thought, the going here was a lot more difficult than anything else I'd attempted so far, maybe not quite rock climbing, but still steep and requiring me to grab hold of a boulder here and and a clump of rabbitbrush there to keep hauling myself along.

Eventually, though, I managed to scramble up those final few feet, and found myself standing on a much more level surface, clearly the main trail. My breath was coming in sharp pants, and I pulled the water out of my pack and drank most of what remained, figuring it should all be downhill from here.

So to speak.

Then I took my bearings, and realized I'd emerged about halfway down the Church Rock trail, not too far from the first set of rock steps... which meant Isaac should be waiting only a few minutes away. I hadn't even noticed the path I'd just climbed when I first passed this way, but I'd been waiting for a sign that I was going in the right direction and hadn't really been paying a lot of attention to every detail of the landscape. Also, more scrubby chamisa grew along the edge of the trail here, and the path was barely noticeable, thanks to the way the brush obscured it.

I stuck the nearly empty water bottle back in my pack, then descended to the spot where the rock stairs began. From up here, I could just barely see the top of Isaac's head. I couldn't exactly tell what he was doing, but something about the angle of his profile told me he seemed to have sat down somewhere, probably on one of the boulders that were scattered here and there on the sides of the trail.

"Hey," I called down, and at once he shifted, looking up toward where I stood.

"Penny?"

"Yep," I said, and couldn't help grinning even though I didn't think he could see me. I hadn't really wanted to admit it to myself, but some-where deep down, I'd been worried that maybe another demon might have come along and tried to attack Isaac as he waited there for me. While he had his own defenses, I honestly didn't know whether he would have been up to such a confrontation.

It seemed those fears had been baseless, however.

"Coming down now," I said. "Just give me a minute."

Descending the rock stairs was actually scarier than climbing them had been, mostly because it felt as though gravity was making its presence felt a lot more strongly than it had during my ascent. However, I made myself go slowly, picking out each step with care, and soon enough I'd reached the bottom.

Isaac was waiting for me there, and let go of one crutch so he could take me by the hand and give me a quick, relieved kiss. "What happened? Did you find anything?"

"Oh, I found something, all right," I replied, then sent a quick glance around us. The spot was completely unoccupied except for Isaac and me, and yet I felt awfully exposed here. "But I think it would be better to get down off this mountain and go back to the hotel before we talk about it."

A lot of men I'd known in the past would have protested, would have asked me to provide some answers right then and there. But because this was Isaac, he only said, "Sure."

I gave him a quick kiss on the cheek. "Then let's get going."

The hike down felt interminably long to me, but in actuality, we were back in my Palisade and headed toward the Hampton Inn within an hour. The whole time, I kept shooting uneasy glances around me, wondering what the hell I would do if a demon suddenly appeared on the road in front of us.

Probably floor it and hope my SUV was sturdy enough to mow down one of the unholy creatures.

But no one stopped us, and we were able to make it back to the hotel without incident. By some unspoken agreement, we both went into Isaac's room. Why there, I didn't know, although I guessed he'd probably placed some warding spells on the space, while I'd been relying on the protection amulet he'd given me and not much more.

"This was hidden in an abandoned mine," I said as I carefully pulled the orb out of my pack, then set it down on the dresser, since that was the closest flat surface. To my relief, the precious artifact seemed to have survived all the jostling just fine —the gems embedded in the cross were intact, and the rock crystal didn't appear to have gotten scratched. "I'm pretty sure the liquid inside is the patriarch's tears. At any rate, the demon I bumped into wasn't too happy about having them splashed on him."

"'Demon'?" Isaac repeated in some alarm, even though it should have been obvious to him that I'd survived the encounter just fine, or I wouldn't be here at all. "What happened?"

While I didn't have much desire to relive the experience, I did my best to recount what had happened when the demon crossed my path, including the way the holy water—or whatever it was—had melted him away in a matter of seconds.

"I'm sure that's why he wanted to take it away from me," I concluded. "No demon would want that kind of weapon in the hands of a mortal."

"Probably not," Isaac agreed. "Do you mind if I take a look at it?"

"Go for it," I replied. "There's something that looks like Latin written on the band around the middle—maybe you can make sense of the inscription."

"I'll give it a try," he said. "Our church switched over to English masses when I was just a kid, but I've retained a little of it."

Since I'd never attended a Catholic service in my life, I'd just sort of assumed that Mass was performed in Latin. Too bad, because it probably would have helped if Isaac were more familiar with the language than he professed to be.

Still, I didn't comment, only waited while he picked up the orb and inspected it closely, eyes narrowing as he scanned the finely engraved letters on the gold band that rested on the equator of the rock crystal sphere.

"Pontifex lacrimae eos qui Legio sunt abluet," he

read aloud, and frowned, amazement...and a little fear...showing in his dark eyes.

"Ponti who?" I said.

Despite the obviously complex emotions that seemed to be crowding his mind right then, he flashed me a quick smile.

"'Pontifex' means the Pope," he explained. "I think it's saying something about the Pope's tears washing away a legion."

"That doesn't mean any sense," I said.

His expression clouded for a moment, and then his eyes lit up. If we'd been living in a cartoon, he probably would have had a lightbulb go off over his head. "The riddle," he said. "'Patriarch' is another way of saying 'pope.' That means...." The words trailed off, and he looked down at the writing on the orb's golden band once again. "No wonder that demon went up in smoke."

I crossed my arms and shot Isaac some serious stink-eye. "If you don't explain what you're talking about right now, I'm seriously going to have a hissy fit."

Although I'd halfway expected him to at least crack a half smile at those words, his expression remained serious. "There's only one explanation," he said. "This orb contains holy water blessed by the Pope himself."

Chapter 13
Seal of Disapproval

"The pope, pope?" I repeated. I supposed the tears' origins explained the fancy packaging —from what I'd seen in pictures, it looked as though the Vatican was as gold-plated as Donald Trump's apartment—but I couldn't quite figure out how the crystal orb had gotten so far from home.

"It's more than that," Isaac said. "Come look at this."

Obediently, I went over to where he stood, the orb still cradled in hands that looked much more reverent now than they had a few minutes ago. He pointed at a few words engraved beneath the larger font, so small it was no wonder I hadn't noticed them before now.

Squinting, I said, "'Peter I'?"

Now Isaac did smile slightly. "Peter the First.

As in, the first bishop of Rome, or the first pope. If this thing is real—and I have no reason to think otherwise, considering the water's effect on the demon you met on the path—then this holy water was blessed by Saint Peter himself."

For a second or two, I could only stare back at Isaac, not sure what I was supposed to do with this new piece of information. Saint Peter? Then that meant....

"Yes," Isaac said quietly. "This orb is more than two thousand years old."

A little shiver went over me. No, I wasn't a religious person, but anyone who wasn't awed simply by being in the presence of such an artifact didn't have much sense of context. Now I understood why the stones set in the cross were smooth cabochons and not fancy faceted gems, and the diamond in its original rough form, since my art history classes had taught me that faceting was a fairly recent invention in the grand scheme of things.

"How in the world did Mina Powers get her hands on something like this?" I asked, and Isaac only shrugged.

"I don't know. Obviously, she wanted to make sure it was hidden somewhere safe, a place where no one would accidentally stumble upon it, but I think the story of how she came across the thing in the first place went with her to the grave."

Along with roughly a million other secrets. I tried not to sigh, since doing so wouldn't change the current situation. "Well, that definitely explains why the demon dissolved so fast. The stuff inside must be like holy water on steroids."

"Definitely," Isaac agreed, even as a frown tugged at his brow. "What worries me is how that demon knew you were coming."

That thought had bothered me, too, although at the time, I'd been more interested in meeting up with Isaac and getting the hell off that mountain trail than dissecting the significance of the encounter. "Maybe once I brought the orb to the surface, it triggered some kind of alarm?"

"Possibly, but if that's the case, wouldn't more demons have come after you once you killed the first one?"

An argument that made sense, even as I gave a little inner shudder at the thought of having to fight off demons right and left as I tried to make my way back to the Church Rock trail. "Maybe," I said. "Or maybe the demons kept a guard posted there, since they knew Mina Powers was in the area when she died, and they wanted to keep watch to see if anyone else ever came that way."

Even as I spoke, though, I wondered if that theory was just a bit implausible. After all, we were talking about a span of thirty-plus years here, not hanging around for an hour or two to see whether someone might return to the scene of the crime.

But Isaac didn't seem to think my speculation was too off the mark. "I could see that happening," he said, then added as I lifted an eyebrow, "Demons are immortal, remember? They don't feel the passage of time the same way we do." A pause, and he asked, "Was there anything special about this demon? Was he just like the others?"

At once, I shook my head. "No. I mean, he definitely looked like a demon, but he was bigger and his features seemed a little more human than the others. And he left this behind after he disintegrated."

I dug in my pocket and produced the bronze medallion, almost forgotten during Isaac's discovery of the true meaning of the riddle Mina had left for me to find.

He took it from me, that same frown pulling at his brows, only more pronounced this time.

"Do you know what it is?" I asked, since he didn't seem inclined to say anything right away.

"No," he replied. "It gives me a bad feeling, though."

Well, that didn't seem too strange, considering the trinket had been left behind by a demon. Still, these days it was easy enough to dig up even the most esoteric information on the internet, so we should be able to solve that particular mystery quickly enough.

"If you want, I could copy the design to make it a little clearer, and then we could—"

I'd been about to say, *We could take a picture and upload it into Google's image finder,* but Isaac didn't let me get that far.

"No, I don't think drawing this thing is a good idea at all," he broke in. "This is some kind of sigil or device, and copying it by hand would be almost like casting a spell of summoning. I think it's better to take it back to Santa Fe and let me scan it on the printer in my home office. Then we can use that image to try to figure out what it is."

Could a spell of summoning even work when the being you were summoning was dead beyond any hope of resurrection? I didn't know, and because this was Isaac's field of expertise and not mine, I decided I wouldn't bother to argue the point.

"What do we do, then?"

He went over to my bag and slipped the orb inside, then turned back to me. "We get out of here," he said. "I can't profess to know all the ramifications of this discovery, but I do know we'll be safer back in Santa Fe."

Good idea. Even though the capital city had only been my home for about a month, I still felt far safer there than I'd been anywhere else, even the home where I'd grown up. Being on the road had made me feel horribly exposed, and this latest demon appearance—even if I had managed to vanquish the creature—only served to remind me that I never knew where the next attack might come from.

"I'll get packed," I said.

We went straight to Isaac's house, and that made me feel better, too. Sure, we'd done our best to protect my adorable little rental, but his home was warded by layers and layers of spells, making it more like the magical equivalent of Fort Knox. If there was a safer place to stash the orb—and to investigate the medallion the demon had left behind—I sure didn't know what it was.

No thought of relaxing after the long drive with a glass of wine and a snack, either. Instead, we went straight to the elevator and descended to his basement workroom, where he took the orb from my purse, swathed it reverently in a length of blue silk he pulled out of a drawer, and then placed it in a big metal cabinet that looked as though it might have once been a gun safe but seemed to be used now to store the most precious of the crystals and other elements he used for his spells and rituals.

A pause as he murmured a few words in

Spanish under his breath—yet another warding spell, I guessed, this one intended to make sure that even if someone managed to penetrate this far into his sanctum, they wouldn't be able to get their hands on the orb—and then Isaac said, "All right. It's about as safe as it's going to be. Let's go upstairs to my office and see what we can find out about this medallion."

So, it was back in the elevator, and then into the room he was using as his office, although I guessed that once it had been intended as a den, since it had a small kiva-style fireplace in one corner, a duplicate of the one in the living room, and a pair of French doors opening onto the patio that encircled the entire ground floor of the house. There was a largish desk pushed up against one wall, its surface covered with papers and stacks of manila folders, and on the wall next to it sat a file cabinet with a big multi-function printer sitting somewhat precariously on top.

Isaac went over to the printer and lifted the lid, and set the medallion on the scanner's surface. A few button presses and a few seconds of waiting for the thing to warm up, and then it hummed away, making a pass of the medallion. As I watched, he got out a thumb drive and inserted it in the USB connection, and then pressed a few more buttons, presumably transferring the file so he could upload it to his computer.

I almost asked why he hadn't just taken a photo of the thing and emailed it to himself, but maybe he didn't want to take the risk of storing something so dubious on his phone. Once again, I was reminded of all the hidden gotchas I didn't know about working with magic, of how there were so many precautions a person needed to take.

Especially when dealing with demons, it seemed.

Thumb drive in hand, he went over to his desk chair and sat down, leaning his crutches against one side of his desk. The computer was an older-looking tower model, very different from my sleek little MacBook Air.

But the old Dell seemed to work just fine, as it woke up pretty quickly and let Isaac transfer the image files from the thumb drive to his desktop. A little more fiddling around—it looked to me as though he was using a VPN to connect to the internet, probably because he didn't want Google to know what we were up to—and then he navigated to a browser I didn't recognize.

However, it seemed to have a lot of the same functions as Google, because it went to an image lookup screen, where he uploaded one of the images he'd just scanned.

Since I was standing behind Isaac's shoulder, watching this whole procedure, I saw the result come back at exactly the same time he did.

"'The seal of Belial,'" I read aloud. "What the hell is that?"

Sounding grim, Isaac replied, "Nothing good."

I put my hands on my hips. "Want to clarify?"

He glanced over at the screen, and then back up at me. "Let's get something to drink first."

After that climb up the mountain and the drive back to Santa Fe, I was definitely in the mood for refreshment with a little more oomph to it than bottled water. "Sure," I said.

We headed into the kitchen, where he put together a fairly respectable charcuterie platter from the contents of his fridge's deli drawer, and also got out a bottle of rosé. "Can you get some glasses, and bring some water, too?" he asked. "I need a drink, but we should probably have water with this, just to be safe."

I nodded, and went ahead and got the requested items, then took them out to the living room. Isaac carried the bottle of wine, since he could manage that even while on his crutches, but I needed to go back to fetch the tray of food.

Within a couple of minutes, we were sitting on the sofa, wine poured, a fire going in the gas fireplace a few feet away. The scene both felt and looked utterly cozy, but I couldn't ignore the little shiver that crawled down my spine as I thought of what was about to come next.

I had a feeling that what Isaac needed to tell me wasn't anything I wanted to hear.

After we'd both drunk a couple of swallows of rosé and had helped ourselves to a few bites of meat and cheese, he said, "Belial is one of the princes of Hell. If that demon you fought was wearing a medallion with his device on it, then that means he must have been working for him."

The piece of smoked gouda I'd just consumed seemed to stir uneasily in my stomach. "What would a prince of Hell want with someone like me?"

A corner of Isaac's mouth lifted, but I didn't see any real mirth in his expression. "Not you particularly," he said. "Anyone who came into possession of the orb. An artifact like that—one that's an even more efficient demon-killing machine than the sword you found outside Cimarron—is something a devil would want permanently out of circulation."

"'Devil'?" I repeated, not sure I was following the argument. "I thought we were talking about demons here."

His mouth tightened. "I'm not an expert, but it's fairly common knowledge that there are hierarchies of demons just as there are hierarchies of angels. There are nine princes of hell—nine devils, of whom Lucifer is only one, although he's the strongest. Belial is one of the others."

This was getting better and better. Worrying about demons popping up on my doorstep had been bad enough. Now I had to throw actual devils into the mix?

"Well, that's great," I said and then took a swallow of rosé, since I didn't know what else to do. "How am I supposed to fight off a devil?"

"With the orb and the sword," Isaac said. But then he let out a breath that belied the calmness of his tone and added, "At least, I assume that's why Mina Powers hid both those objects, so her daughter would find them and use them to defend herself against her diabolical foe."

Suddenly, those few lessons I'd had in sword fighting seemed laughable. Puny little me was supposed to go up against a devil, a being only a few rungs down the ladder from Lucifer himself?

Although the food on the tray had looked good a few minutes earlier, now I was pretty sure if I tried to eat anything else, I'd vomit it right back up. My stomach churned uneasily, and I was glad I'd only had one bite of cheese and one bite of prosciutto.

"I can't fight a devil," I said flatly. "Isaac, this whole thing is crazy. There's got to be some other alternative."

He was silent for a moment, all sorts of thoughts obviously churning away in his mind. Then he lifted his head, reminding me of the way my old dog Rascal would look when he caught an elusive scent on the wind.

"There might be," he said slowly. "This is way beyond me, too. I think we need to call in some experts."

"'Experts'?" I echoed, not sure what he meant. "Like an exorcist or something?"

"Better," he replied, and now he almost smiled. "Penny, have you ever heard of a show called *Project Demon Hunters?*"

Chapter 14
Demon Hunting

To my surprise, I thought I might have heard of *Project Demon Hunters*. The incident had occurred several years earlier, but I vaguely recalled reading about how the show had been abruptly canceled partway through production. Something about one of the people on the crew dying during filming? And wasn't there some footage that had gotten leaked on the internet, something that was supposed to show real-life images of actual demons?

Yes, that was it. The whole thing had blown over eventually, with all the internet sages weighing in and saying the footage was obviously the result of some really good CGI and nothing more, but for a week or two there, the whole world had been speculating as to whether demons were real or not, along with all the metaphysical ramifications involved if the video really proved unearthly creatures like them truly existed.

I related all this to Isaac, and he nodded. "Yes, there was supposed to be a cable TV show, but tragedy kept them from moving forward with it. And there was all that argument about whether the footage that got leaked was real."

Frowning, I said, "I thought it was proven to be a fake, nothing more."

Now he was wearing a Sphinx-like smile I recognized all too well. "That's what they wanted you to think."

The shiver was back, despite the warm sweater I was wearing. I gulped some more rosé and wished the fireplace was a little more effective at generating useful heat. Right then, I felt frozen to the bone. "You're saying that footage was real?"

"Of course it was," he said calmly. "You've seen three different demons now and interacted with them. Are you really going to try to tell me you don't believe in demons?"

As much as I would have liked to do that very thing, I couldn't lie to myself—or to Isaac—like that. "So...you think these *Project Demon Hunters* people might be able to help?"

"If they can't, I don't know who else can," Isaac said. "Michael Covenant and Audrey Barrett —the show's hosts—are now married and living in Pasadena, I think. I can try reaching out on

Michael's website and see whether he has any advice to offer."

Pasadena. Pretty much my old stomping grounds. I wouldn't allow myself the time to reflect on the irony of having an honest-to-God demonologist practically living in my backyard. Then again, when I was living in Rancho Cucamonga, I had yet to learn I was actually a witch, or that knowing a demonologist might actually turn out to be handy.

"What if he says no?" I asked, figuring I might as well leap ahead into worst-case scenarios so I could steel myself against any eventual disappointment.

Isaac didn't even blink. "I doubt he will."

"But if he does?" I persisted.

"Then I suppose I'll try contacting someone at the local diocese for their help." He reached over and stroked my arm very lightly, a gentle touch intended to reassure and nothing more.

All the same, a rush of warmth went through my body, helping to counteract the chill from a few minutes earlier. Even so, I knew I needed to focus. If a prince of Hell really was sending his minions after me to retrieve the artifacts I'd found, then I couldn't allow myself to be distracted by something as silly as physical attraction...even if some part of my brain was telling me that maybe I wouldn't be so distracted if Isaac and

I would just do the deed and stop all this dancing around.

That wasn't going to happen, though. He'd been open with me about a lot of things, including a clear admission that he wasn't quite ready to move things forward on a physical level and that I'd just have to be patient with him. I wasn't going to kid myself and say it was all right, but Isaac deserved my patience, and I knew I'd give it to him...even if my thwarted libido might have a different opinion on the matter.

"But," he went on, "I'm pretty sure Michael Covenant isn't going to turn us down. Chasing demons—or devils—is kind of his thing."

I hoped Isaac was right. A prince of Hell was way above my pay grade.

And that didn't even include having to deal with my quite possibly sociopathic biological grandmother. Anyone who'd put a demonic hit on her own daughter wasn't exactly a candidate for mother of the year.

So far, I hadn't heard a damn thing from Don Tanner, the private investigator I'd hired to dig up whatever information he could find on Mina Powers, although I told myself it had only been a few days since I reached out to him and that I needed to be more patient. Still, the lack of communication frustrated me. If I had more to go on, I might be able to figure out what my biological grandmother was plotting next.

Or maybe she wasn't plotting at all. Maybe her two attempts to send demons after me had failed, and so she'd given up.

Yeah, right.

It seemed a little more plausible that maybe Belial had cut her off at the pass in their mutual pursuit of the artifacts Mina had hidden all those years ago, and that she might be out of the picture entirely. After all, the woman might be a formidable witch, but I kind of doubted she had the magical firepower to go up against a being who'd been around since the beginning of time.

If you believed in that sort of thing, of course. In my particular case, I didn't have much of a choice.

"I'll send Michael Covenant a message after we're done eating," Isaac said. "Whatever happens, we need to keep our strength up."

"I don't think I can eat, Isaac," I told him. "My stomach is all in knots over this."

Once again, he reached over to me, only this time to lay his hand on top of mine and give it a gentle squeeze. "I can understand that. Would you feel better if I contacted him now? You'll need to get my laptop from the office, but—"

"That would help a lot," I said at once, knowing

it was only the truth. I'd never been able to concentrate with unfinished business hanging over my head. Even if this Michael Covenant person took a while to get back to us, I'd still feel better knowing we'd done as much as we could. "Where's your laptop?"

"On the bookcase, lower shelf. You'll need to unplug it."

"Be right back."

I leaned over and gave him a quick kiss, then got up from the sofa and hurried into the office. When I was in here a few minutes earlier, I hadn't even noticed the laptop, but now I saw it was sitting exactly where Isaac had said it would be, quietly charging on the bottom shelf of the bookcase.

It was an HP that clearly had seen a lot of use if the scratches on the case were any indication. Judging by his computer equipment, Isaac was one of those people who would use a device until it dropped in harness.

Well, it's not like he's had a lot of extra cash to throw around these past couple of years, I told myself as I headed back toward the living room. *Not everyone can afford to buy a laptop every time Apple comes out with a new model.*

Not that he appeared too interested in Apple products, judging by both his desktop and laptop computers. Then again, his cell was an iPhone, albeit a few generations older than the one I'd gotten at Best Buy a few weeks earlier in an attempt to avoid my ex-husband's harassing phone calls. True, the calls had stopped soon afterward, thanks to him expiring of a heart attack after watching a demon assume its true form right in front of his eyes, but at the time, I hadn't known that was the reason for his sudden silence.

I sat down on the couch and handed the laptop over to Isaac. "Here you go."

"Thanks."

He opened the lid, entered his password, and then used the same VPN and private browser he'd employed to find the meaning of the sigil on the demon's medallion. A quick search to find the correct URL for Michael Covenant's website, and he navigated over to the contact form and composed a quick note.

A friend of mine and I have stumbled across something that sounds like it's in your field of expertise. I don't want to go into detail here, but it involves he who is a son of worthlessness. You can reach me at 505-555-8799.

I blinked as Isaac sent off the message.

"'Son of worthlessness'?" I said, and he gave me a humorless smile.

"An epithet for Belial," he replied. "Just an easy code to let Michael Covenant know what we've encountered without having to spell out the name explicitly."

That made some sense, I supposed. Even private browsers and VPNs weren't foolproof, although I kind of doubted that demons were too familiar with computer hacking. Probably better to be cautious, though...just in case.

All the same, I couldn't quite prevent myself from lifting an eyebrow. "How do you even know all this, anyway? I thought you were a *brujo*, not a demonologist."

Before replying, Isaac set the laptop down on the coffee table, carefully avoiding the snack tray and our various wine and water glasses. He moved a little closer to me and took my hand, his fingers strong yet gentle against mine.

"I am a *brujo*," he said quietly. "But most witches understand that we're not alone in the universe, that there are both angels and demons who visit this plane. It just makes sense to know more about them so we don't stumble into something we can't handle."

"Know thy enemy?" I asked, and he nodded.

"Exactly. Although angels are more like allies. They're far less likely to meddle with humans than demons are."

Angels and demons. Devils.

Whatever.

My life was so much more complicated than it used to be. All the same, I thought the chaos would be worth it if it meant I could have Isaac Zamora at my side.

I leaned forward so I could pick up my wine glass, and he did the same. Quietly, we sipped rosé together, Isaac remaining silent as though he knew I needed a few minutes to process all of this.

Well, more like a few years, but I'd take what I could get.

The silence lasted only a minute or so, unfortunately. His cell phone rang from inside his pocket, and he put his glass down so he could pull out the phone and look at the number on the home screen. It must have been something he wanted to take, because he immediately swiped the screen to accept the call and then put the iPhone to his ear.

"Isaac Zamora," he said, his voice brisk and businesslike, quite unlike the musing tones I'd heard a minute earlier. A pause, and then he said, "Yes, that's right. No, she's here with me. The house is heavily warded, so—" He stopped there, brows drawing together as he frowned.

The comment about the house being warded made me guess that was none other than Michael Covenant on the phone. Talk about your fast responses. Had he been sitting on his email, hoping something juicy would come through via his contact form?

I didn't know, although I had to guess that his hasty phone call meant we'd stumbled into something even scarier than I'd feared. But because I could only hear Isaac's side of the conversation, I had absolutely no idea what Michael Covenant might be saying to him.

"Okay, I understand," Isaac said at length. "Tomorrow? Sure—I'll text you the address. We're in Santa Fe." Another pause, and he replied, "That should work. See you then."

Then he put down the phone and looked over at me, expression almost blank.

"Well?" I prompted him, since he didn't seem inclined to say anything right away.

"That was Michael Covenant," he said, quite unnecessarily. "He and Audrey are flying out tomorrow and will come over here as soon as they get settled at their hotel."

"They're coming here?" I responded, startled. "He couldn't just give you some advice over the phone?"

"I guess not." Isaac picked up his rosé and swallowed enough that he drained a good deal of the wine in the glass. Not exactly normal behavior for him, and I could only stare as he went on, "He also said it's not safe for you to go back to your house, since it isn't as heavily warded as mine. You'll need to stay here for a bit."

Under other circumstances, I would have been elated to get an invitation to stay at Isaac's house.

But this was being done for safety's sake, not because he really wanted me here.

Time for a few swallows of wine of my own. I drank some rosé before saying, "You really think that's necessary?"

"Michael Covenant seems to think so, and since he's the expert on these sorts of things, I guess we'd better follow his advice." Isaac's expression cleared a bit, and he added, "In a way, this works out just fine. You've already got your luggage and overnight stuff with you, so you won't even need to go back to your house to get anything."

Well, that was true enough...up to a point. We'd come straight here from the hotel in Gallup, and so I definitely had my usual toiletries and so forth waiting in my bags in the back of the Palisade. However, I'd only packed enough for three days at the most, so if I ended up staying at Isaac's house for an extended period, I'd eventually have to go home, if only to get some more clothes.

But we'd cross that bridge when we got to it. In the meantime, I was pretty well set.

"One of the bedrooms upstairs is a guest room," he told me. "Anita—my sister-in-law— comes by once a month to change out the sheets and the towels in the upstairs bath, so you should be pretty well set."

"Sounds good," I managed, even as I did my best to thrust away the disappointment that

stabbed through me at his words. The logical side
of my brain told me it was stupid to have expected
to stay with him in the main bedroom downstairs...

...but I really, really wished he'd made the offer.

Hoping he wouldn't notice anything odd
about my tone, I quickly went on, "Well, I guess I'd
better get my stuff out of the car and take it
upstairs. Is it okay to leave my SUV parked behind
the garage?"

"No, you'd better bring it inside," he said, and
reached for his crutches so he could push himself
up to a standing position. "It's been fine for you to
leave it there for a couple of hours here and there,
but it's technically illegal to block the garage. I'd
hate for you to get a ticket."

I hadn't even thought about that. While
parking enforcement down near the Plaza seemed
pretty intense—probably due to the overall lack of
places to park—I hadn't even realized the alley
behind Isaac's house was patrolled at all.

"And you're sure there's room?" I asked next,
thinking of how big his specially equipped van was
and how much space it must take up in a garage.

And my own Palisade wasn't exactly a Mini
Cooper, either.

"It'll be fine," he assured me. "Come and see
for yourself."

Still feeling dubious, I followed Isaac as he led
me out of the living room and down the short hall

where the powder room was located. I hadn't really gone any farther than that in this part of the house, mainly because I'd never had any need to.

We passed through a largish laundry room with a washer and dryer that looked like the rejects my friends and I had donated to charity after we graduated and needed to get rid of our rental's furnishings, and past that into the garage. Just as Isaac had said, there was a ton of room here. Yes, his van took up one side of the space, but it didn't look as though he used any of the garage for storage, and so there was definitely a spot where my SUV should fit just fine.

Then he pressed the button to open the garage door. It slowly folded up and out of the way, squeaking a little as it went, revealing the Palisade pretty much blocking the entire length of the door.

"There you go," he said.

"Thanks."

I went and got into my vehicle, realizing I'd have to back it up a bit so I could get the correct angle to enter the garage. Luckily, this only took one try—I hated the thought of miscalculating and having Isaac stand there and watch me go back and forth until I got it right, like some kid trying to pass the parallel parking portion of their driver's test—and soon enough, the SUV was parked next to his van. It was a little bit of a squeeze to get out, but not too bad.

That task accomplished, I went around the back of the Palisade and gingerly opened the lift gate just enough so I could get out both his and my bags, since we hadn't bothered to unload anything after we got back to Santa Fe. Still, it wasn't as if we'd packed like Rose boarding the *Titanic,* so I was able to wrangle all the bags unaided.

"Where do you want yours?" I asked.

He made a movement as though he was about to take his duffle bag from me...until he realized it was probably better to let me carry everything than try to untangle its straps from my overnight tote.

"This way."

Once again, he took the lead, this time taking me past the living room and down the hallway where his home office was located. We moved past its door, however, and kept going a few more paces to what was obviously the main bedroom.

"You can just put my duffle bag on the floor," he told me.

If he felt at all embarrassed to have me in the master suite, he didn't show it. I went ahead and slid the duffle bag off my shoulder and set it on the floor at the foot of the bed, which was a big king with a wrought-iron headboard and footboard. It was covered with a white-on-white embroidered duvet and had a pair of pillows that matched the duvet placed up against the headboard, but otherwise, the bed was completely unadorned. In fact, the whole room was like that, spare and elegant, with white walls and wrought-iron fixtures and nothing else in terms of ornamentation except a gorgeously glazed vase filled with autumn leaves sitting on the dark wood dresser.

The whole room felt completely and utterly Isaac to me.

But because I didn't want him to think I was snooping, I quickly turned back to him and said, "The guest room?"

He offered me a faint smile, but I really couldn't tell what he might be thinking. Was he feeling awkward about having me in his bedroom, or slightly embarrassed that he wouldn't be able to take me upstairs to show me the guest quarters?

"Go up the stairs," he said. "The first room on the right is the guest room. Directly across the hall is the bathroom. I wish I could show you, but—"

"It's fine," I said hastily. "Let me just dump this stuff, and then I'll meet you in the living room."

"Sounds good."

He walked with me to the stairs, but then headed for the living room while I made my way up the steps. It felt strange to be coming up here to a part of the house I'd never seen before and one that Isaac barely even used. A while back, he'd told me he could manage to get up here every once in a while, but most of the time he just left it alone, or had one of his brothers fetch something down if it was urgent and he didn't have the energy that day to climb the staircase.

As he'd said, there was a room immediately to my right as I entered the upstairs hall, a nicely furnished guest space with a queen bed, a highboy dresser, and two side tables. The closet was fairly small, but it wasn't as though I had a lot of clothes to hang up in there. In fact, I didn't even bother with trying to get settled in, and instead just dumped my two bags on the floor of the closet and told myself I'd unpack later as I was getting ready for bed.

The bathroom across the hall reminded me of the kitchen, with its green tile and oak cabinets and general air of having been designed sometime before I'd even been born. But everything looked clean and ready to go, and I wondered if Isaac's sister-in-law also wiped down the countertops and the shower when she came by to change out the sheets and towels, or whether he had a cleaning crew to come in and manage that sort of thing for him.

Either way, it seemed as though I'd have a comfortable enough stay here...however long that stay might last.

I went back downstairs to the living room, where Isaac had refilled our wine glasses.

"All settled?" he asked.

"Pretty much," I said as I sat down on the

couch next to him. I surveyed the half-eaten contents of the charcuterie board, then added, "So...are we under house arrest until Michael Covenant and his wife show up?"

Isaac gave me a slight shake of the head. "'House arrest' might be a little extreme, but I did get the impression that he wanted us to stay put. We can order in tonight, and then tomorrow I'll make dinner for all of us. Michael didn't say what time he was going to get in, but I doubt it'll be early in the day."

No, probably not. It wasn't impossible to get a last-minute flight from Albuquerque to Ontario International or vice versa, since I'd had to do pretty much the same thing a few weeks ago to attend Dave's funeral. However, in that sort of situation, you generally didn't get the best departure and arrival times, and almost always had to pay through the nose for the privilege of not planning ahead.

By that point, I'd been around Isaac long enough to know I shouldn't ask whether he was up to making a big meal for all of us. He knew better than I how much energy he had to spare, and besides, if we took it easy tonight and just ordered in Chinese food or whatever and hung out in front of the TV, he should be rested enough after our expedition to Gallup to conjure up some serious kitchen magic.

And actually, even though our reason for sheltering in place was pretty frightening, I had to admit I liked the idea of a low-key evening spent together, followed by the two of us sleeping in the same house. Not in the same bedroom, unfortunately, but I had to hope things would progress to their natural conclusion sooner rather than later.

"That all sounds good," I said, and scooched a little closer to him. Right then, I thought I'd had enough meat and cheese, and would rather indulge in something even tastier.

He seemed to understand, because he reached over and wrapped his arms around me, drawing me close. Our mouths met, and once again I wanted to lose myself in the delicious taste of him, the way he could make me forget everything except Isaac Zamora, how we could create this wonderful little bubble where nothing in the outside world mattered very much.

With any luck, someday I'd figure out how to make those moments last forever.

Chapter 15
Sins of the Father

About midway through the morning—after Isaac had made me the best breakfast burrito I'd ever had, topped with homemade green chile sauce—he got a text from Michael Covenant.

Getting into ABQ a little after 5, it said. *Will get in touch after we're done @ the hotel.*

"Perfect timing," Isaac said aloud to me, since I was standing close by, having just finished the breakfast washing-up. He typed back, *Great. Come over when you're ready. I'm making molé.*

All he got back was a thumbs-up, but that was enough. At least Mr. Covenant hadn't tried to beg off or say that Isaac didn't need to go to all that trouble. Maybe he figured it was the least we could do, considering he was dropping everything to come to Santa Fe and try to help out with our demon issue.

Devil issue. Whatever.

Maybe I was feeling a bit too lighthearted that morning, considering everything that was hanging over our heads. But help was on the way, Isaac and I had had a great make-out session on the couch the afternoon before, and we'd spent a night absolutely undisturbed by any demon intrusions. For all our worries, we seemed to be doing just fine at the moment.

Well, "fine" was a relative term. But the sun was shining, and I just wouldn't allow myself to be too anxious...especially now that I knew Isaac would be making molé for dinner.

True, he'd probably chosen the dish because he knew its preparation would take up a good chunk of the afternoon, but that was all right. Our relationship seemed to grow a little deeper every day, and yet I could tell he didn't want to take any steps that were too significant, didn't want to make promises he couldn't keep. And honestly, I thought I was all right with that. With so many other things to worry about, this just wasn't the time to be making any major moves.

At least, that's what I tried to tell myself.

So, I helped by tidying up and doing some light dusting, that sort of thing, even though Isaac tried to protest that I didn't need to put myself out that way. But I only told him I wanted to help, and that since I wouldn't be of much use in preparing our dinner, the least I could do was make sure the house was ready for company.

I actually was able to provide a little assistance in the kitchen, mostly by chopping up ingredients or by sticking chiles in the toaster oven to get them properly roasted before they went into the sauce. The whole process was much more intricate and complicated than I could have imagined, and gave me a much greater appreciation of all the work that had gone into the molé dishes I'd eaten in the past.

And then Isaac's phone got a ping a little before six, a message that said, *OK to come over?*

By then, it was late enough that a chicken was already roasting in the oven, and the sauce was just about ready. In between all the molé prep, he'd also made beans in his Instant Pot—the most modern gadget in the kitchen—and gotten some rice going on the stovetop as well.

Yes, he sent back. *Dinner's just about ready. See you in about ten minutes then.*

Still nothing about us going to too much trouble, and I allowed myself an inner head shake. For someone involved in something as fringe as demonology, Michael Covenant did seem like a very businesslike person.

"Do you mind setting the table?" Isaac asked then, sounding apologetic. "I sort of have my hands full here in the kitchen."

"Of course not," I told him. "Be glad to."

And since I'd been over to eat at the house often enough during the past month, I knew where everything was kept, and it didn't take me too long to put out four place settings at the long oak table in the dining room, and to set one of the heavy blown-glass wine goblets that matched his dinnerware at each of those places. Because this was company—even if they were here on "official" business—I went ahead and lit the candles at the center of the table.

Just as I was putting away the Aim-n-Flame, the doorbell rang.

"Can you get that?" Isaac asked, spoon paused over the chicken, which he'd just been coating in molé sauce.

"Sure," I replied, since it was obvious he had his hands full.

I hurried over to the door, mind racing with questions about the people who waited on Isaac's doorstep. Yes, I'd seen Michael Covenant's photo on his website—he looked as though he was a few years older than I, with fair hair and intense, unusual gray eyes with hints of gold—but I hadn't seen a picture of his wife on there and so didn't know quite what to expect.

What I hadn't been expecting was a woman right around thirty, casually gorgeous in a girl-next-door sort of way, with long, wavy brown hair and big brown eyes. No wonder they'd wanted to cast her as Michael's sidekick on *Project Demon Hunters*. She definitely didn't look like someone with a Ph.D. in parapsychology.

"Hi," I said quickly, hoping the couple hadn't noticed the way I'd been staring. "I'm Penny Briggs. Come on in."

They stepped inside quickly. I noticed how Michael waited until I'd shut the door and locked it before he held out a hand and said, "Michael Covenant."

"And Audrey Barrett," his wife added. "We really appreciate you and Isaac having us over for dinner."

"It's just safer that way," Michael put in. His gaze moved around the space, but I somehow got the feeling he wasn't looking at the furniture, and instead was doing his best to sense all the wards Isaac had cast, was making sure we really were as protected here as Isaac had said we would be.

Apparently, Michael was satisfied by what he'd detected, because he gave a very small nod of his head.

"But we do thank you," he said. He had a nice voice, just a bit deeper than Isaac's, with the kind of smooth intonation that made it clear why he was in demand to give talks on the paranormal, let alone getting hired to do a cable show on the subject. "It smells delicious."

"And will taste even better," I assured him.

"Isaac's an amazing cook. Why don't you two go ahead and sit down, and I'll see if he needs any help in the kitchen."

"We'd be willing to lend a hand, too," Audrey said, but I only sent her a smile.

"No, we're good," I told her. "You just made a lightning trip from California to see us, so you need to sit and let us treat you like guests."

She gave me an answering smile as she and Michael followed me into the dining room and took their seats. I went ahead into the kitchen, where Isaac had just finished transferring the beans into their fun hand-painted pot.

"Everyone situated?" he asked, and I nodded. "Great—can you take the beans and rice in? I'm just about done with the chicken."

"Sure," I responded, and picked up the side dishes and took them into the dining room. After a quick smile at our guests, I went back into the kitchen and got the tortillas—they weren't home-made, but I knew Isaac always bought them from a local vendor, and they were fabulous—and the platter of chicken, then went back to the dining room.

He emerged from the kitchen, looking a little apologetic. "Hi," he said. "Sorry I couldn't be there to greet you. I'm Isaac Zamora."

If Michael and Audrey were at all fazed by his crutches, they showed no sign of it. They both murmured greetings, and with the introductions out of the way, it was time for Isaac and me to take our own seats and get situated.

"How was your trip?" he asked as he expertly extricated the cork from the bottle of malbec I'd set out earlier.

"Fine," Michael said. "Everything came together pretty fast, which made getting out here a lot easier."

True, traveling from Southern California to New Mexico wasn't quite the same as flying to Australia or something. "Where're you staying?" I inquired.

"At the Inn of the Governors," Audrey said. "It's right downtown, so it's very convenient."

I didn't know the hotel, since I hadn't been in Santa Fe long enough to memorize all the various businesses, but Isaac gave a knowing nod. "It's a nice place," he said. "I'm kind of surprised you were able to get a room there on such short notice."

"I guess they had a cancellation," Michael responded. "But it worked out to our advantage."

Isaac nodded, and the next few minutes were taken up by passing around plates and bowls and making sure everyone got enough to fill their dishes. Audrey and Michael both took their first bites, and their expressions were one of mirrored amazement.

"This is incredible," Audrey said after she was done chewing. "Did you go to culinary school?"

His wasn't the sort of complexion that showed a flush very easily, but I could tell Isaac was pleased by the praise. "No," he replied. "My mother taught me how to cook."

"She's obviously a very good teacher," Michael put in.

Isaac's shoulders lifted just a bit. "I'm sure she would have been glad to hear that."

The way he phrased the sentence made it pretty obvious she was no longer with us, and Michael and Audrey looked just the slightest bit uncomfortable. However, Michael brushed the moment aside, apparently deciding that now the pleasantries had been dispensed with, we could go ahead and get down to business.

"Do you know why you had an encounter with a demon who'd sworn allegiance to Belial?" he asked abruptly, and I set down my fork and reached for my glass of wine.

Something told me I'd need some fortification for the next part of this discussion.

"That's kind of a long story," I said.

"That's fine," Michael replied. His gaze was still focused on me, almost golden in the reflected light of the candles at the center of the table, and it seemed clear he was willing to wait as long as necessary for me to cough up the pertinent facts.

And I'd thought Isaac could be intense at times.

I shot a quick glance over at him, and he sent me a look much more encouraging than the one I'd just received from Michael Covenant.

Well, we'd asked Michael and Audrey to come because we needed their help, and to offer any kind of useful assistance, they needed to know what Isaac and I had been dealing with over the past month and a half.

So I launched into a recounting of the entire tale, starting with finding my mother's eyeglasses in an antique mall in Albuquerque and the resulting visions I'd witnessed, moving on to the story of the enchanted compass and the sword and riddle it had led me to find, and ending at last with the orb buried in the abandoned mine and the demon who'd been waiting to steal it from me.

The story was punctuated with bites of molé chicken and beans and rice, but it still took me a while to get through it, enough that both Isaac and Michael had gotten second helpings of food by the time I was done, even though I still had a good bit left on my plate...probably because I'd been too busy talking to eat very much.

"And so the demon you killed with the orb's holy water was wearing a medallion with the seal of Belial," Michael said, his tone musing.

My shoulders lifted, even as I said, "I assume he

was wearing it, but I don't remember seeing it on him when he confronted me. It was sort of left behind after he...disintegrated."

Audrey glanced over at her husband. She'd been quiet during my recitation, obviously wanting to absorb all the details and not interrupt with questions, but now she said, directing the question toward her husband, "This doesn't usually happen, does it? I mean, actually killing demons rather than just banishing them?"

"No," he said at once, and ran a hand through his longish dirty-blond hair, mussing the chin-length strands. "Even when you and I were fighting all those demons at the Whitcomb mansion, we were just sending them back to Hell."

"The Whitcomb mansion," Isaac repeated in musing tones. "That's the place where the leaked *Project Demon Hunters* footage was shot?"

Michael nodded. "Yes. We managed to banish those demons, but we definitely didn't kill them. I don't know what to say about the orb...or the sword you found. This is unique, in my experience."

Great. I didn't want our experiences to be "unique." I wanted them to be the sort of thing Michael had dealt with dozens of times before, so he'd know exactly what we needed to do next.

"And Belial," he went on, now looking even

more concerned. "I really want to know what trouble he's trying to stir up now."

"'Now'?" I echoed. It sounded as though he and Audrey had tangled with the demon prince before, or at least were familiar with his shenanigans.

The two of them exchanged a weighted look, one that told me there was a lot of history here...the sort of history I wasn't sure I wanted to learn.

Like it or not, though, I had a feeling I was about to get a history lesson.

Michael straightened and set down his fork, then picked up his glass of malbec and took a sip. "A couple of years ago, Audrey and I rooted Belial out of his hiding place in Connecticut and sent him back to Hell."

I blinked, and Isaac shifted in his seat, his expression one of near-disbelief. "In...Connecticut? You mean he was here, on this plane?"

"Yes." Michael paused there and glanced over at Audrey, and she made a very small nod, as though giving him permission to go on. "This is a little complicated. It turned out that Audrey's great-grandfather, Jeffrey Whitcomb, actually summoned Belial years and years ago, giving him permission to possess his body in return for material wealth."

Since I'd already blinked, I couldn't really do that again. All the same, I couldn't quite keep myself from staring at my dinner guest, whose family history sounded just about as murky as mine. "Whitcomb, as in the Whitcomb mansion from the demon footage?"

Audrey's fingers tightened around the stem of her goblet, although she didn't otherwise move. "The same," she replied. "Except I didn't know it at the time. Even after my great-grandfather died, Belial appeared to have stayed on this plane, pretending to be a mortal man. We still don't know exactly what he was up to all that time, but he did have a hidey-hole in Connecticut, an isolated house where he had a permanent gateway to Hell. After Michael and I tracked him down, we banished him and destroyed the spell circle, making sure he'd never be able to come back here."

"Well," Michael said heavily, "at least we *thought* we'd banished him permanently. Now, I'm not so sure."

I looked over at Isaac, who seemed just about as perplexed as I was. "But that wasn't Belial I bumped into outside the mine, was it? I just thought that demon had to be a servant of his."

"Oh, it wasn't Belial," Michael said at once. "I mean, you've obviously got some high-powered holy water in that orb you found—and I'd love to take a look at it after dinner, if that's okay—but I don't know whether it alone would have been enough to kill a lord of Hell that quickly. We had to drown the bastard in an entire pond full of holy water, and even that was only enough to send him back to his plane, not actually kill him."

A pond of holy water? I wondered how the hell —pardon the expression—they'd managed that particular feat.

It seemed Michael wasn't done, because he went on, "No, I'm sure the demon you killed must have been his servant. It's still worrisome, because about six months after we banished him, Belial tried again to come to this plane and wreak havoc, and it took a whole team of us—including an earthbound angel and my friend Will, who's an Episcopal priest—to send him packing again. That time, though, we all thought we'd wounded him badly enough that he'd be licking his wounds for at least a century or so."

An angel? My head wanted to start spinning again, but I really didn't have time for that. Instead, I reached for my wine and had a healthy swallow, followed by another.

"So, what does it mean that he's interfering again?" Isaac asked, and Michael shot him a grim smile.

"Nothing good," he said.

Chapter 16
Banished and Vanished

"Well, what are we supposed to do, then?" I asked as I did my best to ignore the sinking sensation in my stomach. Because Michael and Audrey were company, and because we'd just met, I tried not to sound too annoyed, but I could tell a lot more frustration leaked out around the edges than I'd intended. "Just sit around and wait for more of Belial's minions to show up?"

"Of course not," Michael replied, his tone also a little too sharp. He paused for a beat, then went on, his voice more even now, "We've beaten the bastard before, and we'll beat him again. I think the most important thing is to figure out what he's up to, and what any of this has to do with you, Penny." His gray eyes glinted at me, sharp as steel in the candlelight. "Tell me what you know."

This part of the story I'd mostly skipped over, figuring it was better to only provide the outlines of my admittedly weird personal background and stick to the stuff that actually involved demons. "Not a lot," I said. "I have a P.I. working on it, trying to see if he can dig up any more stuff about my biological mother's family. About all I do know right now is that her name was Mina Powers, and she supposedly came from Boulder, Colorado. I—"

"Colorado?" he broke in, and I nodded, wondering why that aspect of the story should be so important.

Across the table from me, Audrey shifted uneasily in her chair. Of course, I didn't know her very well, and yet I could have sworn I'd seen a flicker of real fear in her eyes at the mention of the Rocky Mountain state.

Michael sent her a sideways look and her shoulders lifted, even as nervous fingers played with the napkin in her lap.

"It could just be a coincidence," she said, and he tilted his head ever so slightly.

"I don't believe in coincidences."

"What could be a coincidence?" Isaac asked, now sounding almost impatient...for him.

Well, no one liked being left out of the loop, which was exactly how I felt right then. I had to believe he shared that same sentiment, judging by the tone of his voice.

"Colorado," Michael replied after another of those half glances at his wife, as though asking her permission to be the one to answer Isaac's question. "Belial had another one of his properties there, in a place called Idaho Springs. It's about an hour outside Denver...and not that far from Boulder."

Damn it, there went another of those annoying little chills down my spine. I knew it wasn't the temperature, because Isaac kept his house fairly warm. No, it was just my body telling me it really didn't like hearing all this stuff.

"So, what?" I demanded. "You're saying there's a connection between my mother's family and Belial himself?"

"It's possible," Michael replied, obviously unruffled by my sharp tone. "I don't have any evidence, of course, but you've had demons tell you in their own words that your maternal grandmother summoned them to do her dirty work, so it's obvious to me she doesn't have a problem traveling on the dark side of the tracks, so to speak. Maybe she made deals with Belial, or maybe it'll turn out that there's no connection at all. It's just something you might want to keep in mind."

Considering her actions had already landed her on the list of people who should be going straight to Hell the second they departed this mortal coil, I knew I wouldn't even bother protesting that the woman in question would never run the risk of trafficking with a high-level demon like Belial. Anyone with the utter lack of morals or human decency to have the guts to kill her own daughter probably wouldn't scruple at making a deal with a devil, if not *the* Devil.

"Duly noted," I said, and sipped some more of my wine. "But really, that's all I do know. I heard from an agent at the FBI that Mina Powers had quarreled with her mother and then left town...at least, that's what the police report said...but there weren't any other details regarding her disappearance, and no information about the family itself. That's what I have the private investigator working on."

"I'm not sure he'll find much," Michael told me.

"Why would you say that?"

"Because anyone who dabbles in the kind of dark magic your biological grandmother seems to be involved in would make sure she looked squeaky clean on the surface. I have no doubt that all her friends and neighbors think she's a fine, upstanding woman."

I must have made a disbelieving sound, because Audrey put in, "No, it's true. Belial possessed my grandfather for years, and he did very well for himself. Eventually, he ended up in a sanatorium...

but that was only because Belial jumped bodies into Jeffrey Whitcomb's son and basically used his powers to swap their appearances. The man who died in that sanatorium was the son, not Belial."

My eyes widened, even as Isaac asked, "*That* was your grandfather?"

Audrey shook her head—and drank some of her own wine, as if she thought doing so might help to wash away those dark recollections. "No, Jeffrey Whitcomb had daughters as well. One of them was my grandmother. She moved to California sometime in the 1940s, as far as I've been able to tell. My mother died a few years ago, or I'd try to find out if she knew anything more about why her mother relocated to the San Gabriel Valley."

Although Audrey had spoken matter-of-factly enough, I thought I could still hear the echoes of sorrow in her tone. Since she was around my age or maybe just a little younger, I had to believe her mother must not have died of natural causes, that there must have been some kind of tragedy to take her away so young.

"But Belial decided he wasn't done hanging out on this plane," Michael said, picking up the threads of the story...and probably doing his best to deflect any unwanted questions about Audrey's mother. "He assumed Jeffrey Whitcomb's appearance again, since by that time, anyone who'd known the original Whitcomb was probably dead. What exactly he did during all those years, we're not really sure, but it's not too much of a stretch to believe he might have crossed paths with your grandmother, Penny, since she was dabbling in dark magic and seems to have lived not too far away."

"I'd say she did more than dabble," I observed wryly, and picked up my fork so I could have another bite of my amazing but sadly neglected molé chicken. "Or I guess I should say 'does,' since it's pretty clear she never stopped summoning demons."

Isaac sent me an encouraging smile, even as he said, "But it has been pretty quiet the past couple of weeks."

"Well, until I ran into that demon outside Gallup." I looked back over at Michael and asked, "Do you think she might have sent him? Isaac and I have been trying to figure out how that demon even knew I was there, but...."

I let the words trail off, since our discussions on that topic had been anything but conclusive. Expression thoughtful, Michael was silent for a moment before he responded, "I suppose it's possible. Or rather, she could have summoned a demon to keep an eye out for someone from her bloodline. It might not have been the orb at all."

That was a wrinkle I hadn't even thought of. Isaac's brows drew together, and I said, "That's a thing?"

"Oh, sure," Michael replied casually, as though this complication was no big deal. "That's probably how the previous demons tracked you down. I don't pretend to understand how it all works, because this is something I've only started researching since Rosemary—a friend of ours— was shown to have powers that came from a long line of witches. Anyway, each witch family has a slightly different kind of magic, something that a supernatural creature like a demon could use to sniff them out, so to speak. Sort of like witchy DNA, I guess."

When we'd first met, Isaac had told me much the same thing—how every family of witches used a slightly different kind of magic, something that was handed down from generation to generation. Sometimes the thread would be lost, and people wouldn't even realize they'd been born with those sorts of powers, would only think they were slightly psychic or maybe that they were just lucky or whatever.

However, he'd never mentioned that my partic- ular brand of magic was the very reason why I'd been so easy to track once my powers began to blos- som...probably because he hadn't even known such a thing was possible. At least he'd been quick to make sure I was protected by a cloaking spell, although that particular enchantment had been proven ineffective in the end.

"But why in Gallup?" Isaac asked. "Why not come after Penny here in Santa Fe?"

"Because she's more protected here," Michael answered at once. "Both your houses are warded, right?"

Isaac nodded. "Multiple times over. And there's a cloaking spell on Penny's place."

"Then that's why. They couldn't sense her until she left town."

Some of that explanation made sense...and some didn't. "Why didn't they jump on us the second we left the city limits, then?" I asked. "Or come after me all the times I've driven down to Albuquerque, or when I had to go back to California recently?"

To my surprise, it was Audrey who responded to my plaintive questions. "Because demons aren't infallible. They're not omniscient or omnipotent, even if they might be scary as hell...so to speak. Because you're so protected when you're here in Santa Fe, it takes a while for that protective bubble to evaporate, if you know what I mean. Once it was gone, then they'd be able to sense you. It's not instantaneous."

Her explanation made me feel a little bit better.

I hated to think I'd be stuck here permanently, lovely as Santa Fe might be. At least this way, I could still take little day trips here and there until we got all this figured out.

"Also," Michael went on, clearly wanting to add to what his wife had just said, "demons operate in darkness, in stealth. They're not going to pounce on you in a crowded airport or any place that's at all public."

Again, that clarification made a lot of sense. There wouldn't have been any opportunity for a demon to attack me during my trip to California, since I'd been surrounded by people pretty much the whole time. Both times they'd gotten to me, it had been when I was alone in my own house...and when I'd made a couple of pretty colossal mistakes, first by getting lured by the "honey pot" the demon Malphas had set out, and then by letting the second demon right into my house on Halloween. True, I'd thought he was a little girl dressed up as Merida from *Brave* as his trick-or-treating costume, but still, I should have known better than to let anyone over my threshold, no matter how innocent they might have appeared on the surface.

Maybe it wasn't so much that my horrible grandmother had let up for the past few weeks, but more that I simply hadn't given her the opportunity to sic one of her minions on me.

"I know this all sounds pretty grim," Michael added. "But we'll find a way out of it somehow. In the meantime, though, I really would like to take a look at the treasures you found. They might provide a few more clues as to how to fix your demon problem."

Unless "fixing" that problem meant going around armed with an orb and sword, and killing any demon that crossed my path, I wasn't sure how those two items were going to solve anything. Instead of answering directly, though, I glanced over at Isaac. This was his house, and the items were stored in his basement; it was his call as to whether he wanted to take Michael and Audrey down there to play show and tell.

Apparently, he'd decided our guests need to know as much as possible—and that we'd all probably eaten as much of our dinner as we intended to —because he said at once, "Sure, that's a good idea. Let me show you."

He reached for his crutches and maneuvered himself up to a standing position, and the rest of us rose from our seats as well. For just a second, Audrey looked at the uneaten food on the table, probably wondering whether she should say something about packing it up and putting it in the refrigerator before we embarked on our little trip to the basement, but I gave her just the slightest shake of my head. I doubted we'd be down there long enough to cause any real damage, and I'd take care of the leftovers once we were back upstairs.

It seemed like she got the message, because she remained silent as we headed over to the elevator and got in. As the door shut, I wondered whether the thing was even up to the challenge of carrying four adults, but since Isaac didn't say anything and he probably knew the machine's capacity better than anyone else, I decided to keep my mouth shut.

Soon enough, we reached the basement and got out. Michael and Audrey both seemed impressed as they looked around the space, at the long work tables with their various glass vials and mortars and jars of ingredients, at the shelves crowded with more of the materials needed for magic working—herbs and dried flowers, oils and salts and crystals and all sorts of books.

"In here," Isaac said as he made his way over to the gun safe-turned-magic cabinet, and then spun the dial to open the door. Inside still rested the sword in its tooled-leather scabbard, as well as the orb, wrapped in protective blue silk.

He pulled out the orb first and set it on the nearest worktable before removing its shroud of sky-colored silk. Audrey let out a soft sound of amazement, while Michael's dark brows—much darker than his hair, although I could tell he hadn't done anything on purpose to lighten it—pulled together.

"It's beautiful," he said.

"And deadly," I replied. "Or at least, deadly if you're a demon."

"Do you mind if I pick it up?"

"Go ahead," I said. For a second, I wondered if I should tell him about the way it had glowed faintly when I touched it. But then I decided to remain silent and see if it would do the same thing in response to his touch.

Apparently not, because it didn't change at all when he reached out and lifted it carefully in both hands, then peered more closely at the writing on the golden band at the center. "Does that really say 'Peter I'?"

"Yes," I replied. "Obviously, we don't have any way to confirm that it really is filled with holy water blessed by Saint Peter himself, or whether someone put that inscription there to make its contents seem more powerful than they really were, but...."

"But it's pretty effective at killing demons, no matter where it really came from," Isaac put in. He sent Michael a searching look. "What do you think?"

"I think it looks authentic," he said. "Unfortunately, there's no real way to determine how old the metal and the gems are, but the workmanship is consistent with items dating to that period. You can tell by the cabochon stones, by the way the bezels are formed, the shape of the lettering."

"That could all be faked, couldn't it?" I asked, trying not to sound too dubious.

He shrugged. "Yes, but what you can't fake is the effect it has on demons, and it seems as though it's pretty good at performing that particular task."

Since I couldn't really argue with his comment, I only tilted my head slightly and waited for him to go on with his assessment of the orb.

"So, I think it's probably safe to assume it's authentic, or at least authentically antique and filled with some kind of special holy water, even if whoever created it wanted you to think it was blessed by Saint Peter himself rather than a regular old pope." His gaze moved to the sword, still resting on a shelf inside the safe. "Is it okay if I take that out?"

"Sure," Isaac replied.

Michael went over to the safe and carefully lifted the sword from its perch, and then brought it to the table where he'd just set down the orb. A moment to unsnap the fastenings that kept the blade secure in its sheath, and then he pulled it out.

The basement was lit by fluorescent lights, harsh and not particularly friendly. They danced along the length of the slender blade, showing the delicate, barely visible marks left behind on the metal by whoever had forged it.

"We thought it might be new, something that Mina Powers had made especially for her," I said, since Michael didn't seem inclined to speak, but only kept turning the sword this way and that.

What he was looking for, I didn't know. Isaac and I had already inspected the thing top to bottom, had even heated it up in the fireplace to see if there were any hidden letters or runes written on the blade, but we hadn't found a damn thing.

"No, I think it's older than that," Michael said after a long pause. "It's in very good shape, but there are some scratches on the hilt, and something tells me it's not a modern blade."

"'Something'?" I repeated skeptically. For a supposed expert, he was being pretty vague.

Luckily, he didn't seem too offended, and even smiled slightly. He looked like a completely different man when he did that and I could see why Audrey had fallen for him, even if my current tastes ran to something a bit darker and more exotic.

Like Isaac.

"Magic isn't an exact science," he said, echoing what Isaac had already told me weeks earlier. "Sometimes, all we have to go on is a feeling...an itch, if you like. And I'm getting the feeling that this sword has been around for a while. I can't tell you who made it, or where...but I think I can tell you why."

"Which is?" I asked, even though something told me I already knew the answer.

Michael glanced over at Isaac and Audrey before returning his attention to me. His unusual gray-gold eyes glimmered in the cool light from the fluorescent fixtures overhead.

"To kill demons, of course."

Chapter 17
All in the Family

"It's so small, though," Audrey said as she stared at the sword, and I sent her an ironic smile.

"Should I make a comment about how size doesn't matter?"

Isaac's mouth quirked, and even Michael looked amused. However, his tone was serious enough when he spoke again.

"Penny's already killed a demon with it, so clearly it's up to the task." He paused, gaze moving toward the sword for a moment, as if he wanted to measure it with his eyes. "And I'm fairly certain it's the size it is because it was designed to be carried by a woman."

"'A woman'?" I repeated. Yes, that theory made a lot of sense, because we'd already proven that Isaac couldn't hold the sword very easily, thanks to the dimensions of its hilt. His hand was simply too big.

"Why a woman?" Audrey asked.

"Because the vast majority of witches are women, and only someone with special powers would even have a chance when going up against a demon."

At once, comprehension lit up Audrey's big brown eyes, and Isaac nodded as well, as though Michael's pronouncement settled a question he'd been pondering for a while.

And I probably should have come to that same conclusion a while back, since Michael's speculation really wasn't all that out there. Maybe I could have excused myself by remembering that I'd only just learned magic even existed a month ago, and so it wasn't something I'd been steeped in my entire life.

"So, the sword and the orb are supposed to work together to kill a big baddie like Belial?" I asked.

"Possibly," Michael replied. Now he didn't seem quite as sure of himself; his gaze moved back to the sword and the orb and remained there for a moment, as if he was doing his best to measure their fighting capability. "For that sort of confrontation, it would probably require two witches working together, since I think it would be kind of hard to hold on to the orb while trying to stab a demon with your other hand."

He had a point there. The orb fit in the palm of my hand, true, but it was still bulky enough that I couldn't quite close my fingers around it. Trying to maintain a grip on the thing while engaging in hand-to-hand combat with a demon at the same time would require a level of skill I knew I didn't possess, even if I did have a couple of sword-fighting lessons under my belt by that point.

"That would be difficult," Isaac said, "since there's no guarantee you would even have two witches from the same family who would be capable of doing such a thing. Witch talent doesn't always breed true."

"Not all the time," Michael agreed, "but some-times it does. We know a family like that where all three daughters are very strong."

One of whom must be the Rosemary he'd briefly mentioned, even if I could tell he really didn't want to talk about her—or her witch sisters —very much.

"Well, that's all fine and good," I said, now crossing my arms. I was wearing a sweater, but the basement still felt way too cold, since Isaac hadn't switched on the wall heater when we came down here. "But there's only one of me, so if I'm really supposed to defeat Belial with the orb and the sword, then I'm going to have to learn how to handle both of them at the same time."

Michael didn't reply right away, only narrowed his eyes in thought for a moment. Then he said, "Are you sure about that?"

"Sure about what?" I countered.

"Sure that there's only one of you."

When it came to my biological family, I wasn't sure about a lot of things. However, the private investigator's probing had shown mine was one of a batch of only five eggs that Mina Powers had donated, and just two of them had been used—the one my parents had used to conceive me, and one that had apparently conceived Luke Jackson, a man whose existence I hadn't even known about until my father told me about my half-brother last week.

Unless, of course, Mina had managed to donate eggs somewhere else, which didn't seem very likely. The only fertility clinics in New Mexico back then had all been located in Albuquerque, and since the entire process took at least a month, it wasn't as though she could have been leaving donations all over the state. Also, the mere fact that she'd died in that canyon outside Gallup meant she obviously hadn't made it wherever she'd been planning on going.

Was it possible she could have used two different clinics in Albuquerque, though? Again, I thought that was kind of a long shot. Women prepping for that sort of procedure were given quite a few separate medications to increase their egg production and were monitored pretty closely. I supposed it was remotely possible she'd gone to two different clinics and had simply tossed the drugs she'd been prescribed from one of them, but I honestly didn't know whether that would even work.

"I'm pretty sure," I said. "At least, I know I'm not a twin. Whether or not Mina Powers donated eggs somewhere else is something that would be pretty hard to determine. Anyway, considering how my bio-grandmother has been trying to hunt me down—and how the man who was the result of one of Mina's other donations turned up mysteriously dead about six months ago—I wouldn't place much money on such a person's odds of survival right now."

As soon as I mentioned my half-brother, Michael Covenant's gaze sharpened. "You had a sibling? What happened to him?"

Because I'd never met the man, I really couldn't think of Luke Jackson as a sibling. My only real brother was Cade, now drinking his way through his sophomore year at USC. "Well, biologically, I had a half-brother from one of Mina's other eggs," I replied, "but I never even knew he existed until a few days ago. He died of a suspicious heart attack not too long after he moved to Denver."

"Colorado again," Michael murmured, and I got the impression he hadn't necessarily meant those words to be said aloud. "Do you think there's a connection to your grandmother?"

I looked over at Isaac, and his shoulders lifted a fraction of an inch. We'd already discussed this topic and hadn't reached any concrete conclusions, mostly because we still lacked so much evidence.

"Possibly," I said. "Isaac and I thought maybe she realized who Luke Jackson was once he got close enough, but then she figured out he didn't have any powers and decided to get him out of the way, for whatever reason. I'll admit that I don't completely understand the reasons behind killing someone who couldn't possibly have presented any kind of threat to her, but then again, most of the woman's thought processes don't make a lot of sense to me. She seems as though she must be batshit crazy."

Michael's jaw hardened. "Oh, I don't think she's crazy...at least, not in the conventional sense of the word."

"She clearly exhibits sociopathic behavior, based on what you've told us," Audrey said, her tone almost clinical. In a way, I appreciated that; it felt a lot better to discuss the topic with some detachment rather than force myself to remember at every step that this woman was supposedly my blood kin. "But many sociopaths are able to function just fine in society without anyone being able to tell there's something about them that makes them separate from most of humanity. Just because we can't completely understand what she's doing because our minds don't work that way doesn't mean there isn't still some logic behind her actions."

That kind of logic I could do without.

"I suppose so," I said, knowing how grudging those words must have sounded. "But I'm pretty sure that Luke Jackson and I were Mina Powers' only offspring. Which means I guess I need to learn how to sword fight while juggling an orb."

My laconic remark got me a couple of chuckles from Audrey and Isaac, although Michael looked deadly serious. I had a feeling that was his default expression.

"I hope it won't come to that," he said. "The good news is that the sword and the orb are definitely safe down here, and I can't think of a better place to keep them hidden. As for where Mina Powers found them in the first place...."

He stopped there, expression perplexed...and I had to guess that Michael Covenant was one of those people who hated unanswered questions.

I didn't much like them, either, but since I'd been wondering the same thing ever since I found the sword several weeks ago, at least I was used to having an unsolved mystery bouncing around in my brain. My biological mother might have been an extremely talented witch, and yet she still didn't seem like the sort of person someone would have trusted with such valuable...and magical...items.

"We may never know," Isaac said calmly. "And we have to find a way to be okay with that. As it is, I'm just relieved the artifacts will be safe here. I've done everything I could to make sure they're protected, but, considering everything Penny and I have faced over the last month or so, I had my doubts whether all those safeguards would really be enough."

"I don't think anyone could have done any better," Michael assured him, words that helped to relax me a bit. Michael Covenant didn't seem like the kind of guy who would offer false praise. "And I'll admit I was worried...until I came down here and sensed all the wards you have in place on that safe. So, that's at least one thing we don't have to worry about."

Leaving about a million others, but right then, I figured I'd take what I could get.

"Good," I said. And because it seemed as though Michael was ready to hang out in the base-ment and keep discussing possibilities, even though there wasn't much else to look at when it came to the sword and the orb, I added, "It's cold down here—can we go back upstairs? I'm sure Isaac would be fine with you coming back to take a second look at this stuff if you need to."

Michael appeared almost nonplussed by my suggestion, but Isaac, bless him, said, "I should have turned on the heater. But Penny's right—it is chilly in here, and, as she said, if you think of something else you need to check, I'd be happy to let you come back and inspect the sword and orb any time you need."

"That sounds like a good idea," Audrey said, and twined her arm through her husband's. "It's been a long day, and I'm beat."

Because there wasn't any real way he could argue—at least, not without looking like a jerk—Michael nodded. "Of course. I have some research I want to do, now that I've seen the artifacts and heard your story. There may be some angle I haven't thought of yet."

"Sounds good," I replied. It was on the tip of my tongue to add that he needed to be careful in his internet searches, but then I told myself that someone like Michael Covenant hadn't just fallen off the turnip truck. While he seemed a little single-minded to me, he was also good at what he did, and obviously knew how to be discreet.

Isaac rewrapped the orb in the length of silk and returned it to the gun safe, and then slid the sword into its sheath and set it down on the shelf right above the rock crystal sphere. After closing the safe, he murmured a few words under his breath, no doubt resetting the protection charm on the cabinet.

With that handled, we all headed back to the elevator and went upstairs. The remains of our dinner were looking pretty forlorn, and Audrey said, "Do you need any help cleaning up?"

"No," Isaac and I said in unison, and I couldn't help cracking a grin. "We're fine," I continued. "Most of this stuff is going straight into the fridge. Besides, you're our guests. You came all this way to help out, and you've done a lot to relieve some of our worries."

For a second or two, she looked as though she might protest, but a quick look from her husband seemed to tell her she needed to let it go. "Well, thank you for a lovely dinner," she said. "I'm glad we could help."

"And I'm going to keep working on this," Michael put in. "Luckily, you caught us just as we got back from a lecture tour, so we don't have any real commitments until after the first of the year. Not that we plan to stay that long," he added hastily after intercepting an alarmed glance from Audrey. "But we did book the room for a week, just to be safe."

Whereas I had storyboards to work on, and Isaac had a store to run. True, he didn't need to be back until Monday, giving us another precious day off, and my storyboards weren't due until the first of December, but that didn't mean I could ignore the rest of my life to work on the puzzle of the orb and the sword.

But now that Michael and Audrey were here, maybe I wouldn't have to.

We walked them to the door and said our good-byes. Afterward, Isaac and I both headed back to the dining room to work on clean-up. Or rather, I told him I would handle it, since I could tell by the way he seemed to drag his crutches along that he'd over-extended getting the elaborate meal prepared and then entertaining our guests, and he just didn't have any energy left.

Being Isaac, he tried to protest, but I told him to sit down in the living room and rest, and that I'd whack him over the head with one of his crutches if he so much as lifted a single fork from the table. To my relief, he grinned at the silly threat and left me to it.

The pile of dishes did look kind of scary, but I triaged everything—making sure all the leftovers were safely stored in the fridge first, and then moving on to the plates and glasses and cutlery—and within the half hour, the table was cleared, the dinnerware and wine glasses and silverware were deposited in the dishwasher, and the pots and pans left to soak in the sink.

When I came back out to the living room, Isaac

was sitting quietly on the sofa with the fireplace going, but he hadn't turned on the TV or even any music. Instead, he was just resting there, eyes half-closed, although I could tell he wasn't asleep.

"You shouldn't have done all that," he said, and I lifted a hand, waving his protest away.

"I wanted to," I replied. "You did all the cooking, so it's only fair that I did the clean-up."

"You chopped," he said with a tired smile.

"Not the same thing."

I sat down next to him and scooched over so I could rest my head on his shoulder. He was far too tired for me to initiate any intimacies, but it still felt good to be there next to him, to feel the warmth of his body and smell the clean, aromatic scent of whatever shampoo he used.

"What do you think?" I said at last.

"About what?"

"Michael Covenant. Do you really think he'll be able to help us?"

Isaac didn't reply for a moment, so I waited, feeling the rise and fall of his chest as he took calm, regular breaths. Then he said, "I think so. Or at least, I hope so. He's already provided a few insights that neither of us had thought of, so if nothing else, it's helping to have some fresh eyes on the situation."

Fresh eyes that only seemed to bring up more problems. However, I didn't say anything about that, mostly because experience had taught me that a lot of the time, you had to fight your way through this kind of thorny thicket before you could find the sleeping princess in the castle.

I wasn't looking for a princess, though. All I wanted was to find a way to make sure I'd never have to worry about my evil grandmother—or Belial, or any other princes of Hell who decided to show up and complicate my life even further—ever again.

"Fingers crossed," I said. We were both quiet for a few moments, content to sit there in silence and enjoy simply being in each other's presence, glad for this time when we could be peaceful after the hustle and bustle of our day. I wished all our time together could be like this, just two people doing what they could to explore the connection that had blossomed so unexpectedly between them.

Or maybe not so unexpectedly. I'd never been the sort of person to believe in love at first sight, or to think there was only one person out there for you. All the same, I couldn't deny there was something special between Isaac and me, a spark that had ignited pretty much the moment I laid eyes on him. And although he hadn't come right out and said it, I knew deep down that he'd experienced pretty much the same thing.

That had to be what was keeping him around. Most of the men I'd known would have run for the hills at the appearance of that first demon, and would never have stuck around to help me unravel the mystery of Mina Powers and her terrible mother, or gone along on our little expeditions to find the artifacts she'd left behind.

Clearly, Mina had expected me to pick up those weapons and use them to defend myself, and possibly do much more. Had she been so certain the eggs she'd donated would conceive women with witchy powers strong enough to take on such a burden?

It seemed so. Obviously, her own magic had to be pretty damn strong, or she would never have been able to keep those items secret for so many years, just waiting for the right person to stumble over them.

No, not stumble. Be drawn to them, because I was a lodestone, the same as she had been.

Isaac's hand moved, rested on my knee. "It's going to be all right," he said quietly.

"You're sure about that?"

"As sure as I can be about anything."

I shifted so I could gaze up into his face. His dark eyes were warm and yet concerned at the same time. Not about whatever might happen next, I thought, but that I might allow my own doubts to get in the way, might falter when I needed to be strong.

Well, I wasn't about to let that happen. I might

not know what was waiting around the bend for me, whether it was Belial or some other demon, but I did know one thing.

Whatever came next, I'd face it with Isaac at my side.

Chapter 18
Shop 'Til You Drop

W e went to bed soon after that, sharing a brief goodnight kiss before I headed upstairs. As much as I might have wished for more, I knew both of us were pretty wiped out, and once again I had to remind myself that good things came to those who waited.

I just wished I knew exactly how long that wait was going to last.

Around ten the next morning, after Isaac and I had showered and had breakfast and generally gotten ready for the day—even if I wasn't sure what we were going to do with it—he got a text from Michael Covenant, asking if he could come back over sometime during the day and take another look at the orb and the sword.

Audrey would like to go and do some shopping and exploring, though, he added. *She was wondering*

if Penny would like to go with her. As long as they
stay around downtown, it should be perfectly safe.

That sounded like a fabulous idea to me. I
knew I didn't have much to contribute to a second
inspection of the magical objects, and being able to
hang out with a woman around my own age and
act as though I didn't have a care in the world felt
like it would be just what the doctor ordered.

"Do you really think it will be okay?" I asked
Isaac after he'd relayed the contents of the message
to me, adding wistfully, "It would be nice to get
out for a bit."

"I think it'll be fine," he replied at once. "After
all, you've been going about your business here for
weeks without any issues. Like Michael said, you
have a ton of protection spells wrapped around
you, and demons generally don't like to cause
trouble in public places."

I leaned over and kissed him on the cheek, glad
that he hadn't tried to act all clingy and get me to
stay at the house with him. Yes, Isaac was one of the
most independent people I'd ever met, but I'd had
enough bad experiences with Dave that I was still a
little gun-shy.

"Then tell Michael that would be great."

Isaac sent over the response and waited for a
moment. His phone pinged again. After glancing
down at the screen, he said, "Audrey wants to meet
for lunch at La Plazuela at noon."

On a Sunday, the restaurant would probably be busy, but since it wasn't the height of tourist season anymore, maybe we wouldn't have to wait too long for a table. "Tell her that would be fine."

Even as I spoke, though, I wished I didn't have such a meager assortment of clothes with me at the moment. My pretty wool coat was still back at my rented house, and I mostly had jeans and thermal tops to choose from.

But there was the one nice sweater I'd worn to Isaac's and my dinner in Gallup, and since I'd only put it on for that one meal and hadn't worn it otherwise, I guessed it would do well enough. With jeans and boots, it should be passable for lunch and shopping.

"And what are you boys going to do for food?" I asked after Isaac had sent my confirmation over to Michael and it looked as though everything was set for our girls' day out.

His eyes got those amused crinkles at the corner I loved so much. "Oh, I suppose we'll scrounge something for lunch after Michael is done looking over the artifacts a second time. There's stuff to make sandwiches, or we can have leftovers if he's up for molé a second day in a row."

Considering how good everything had been at dinner the night before, that didn't sound like too much of a hardship to me. But that would be for the guys to decide.

I excused myself to go upstairs and change into the sweater and a nicer pair of boots, then applied a bit more makeup than the mascara and lip gloss I'd put on earlier when I was envisioning a quiet day at home with Isaac. We hadn't made any real plans, both of us realizing that Michael and Audrey might reach out again, even if it was only to do some sightseeing.

But Michael was all business, apparently, and since Isaac was much more knowledgeable about all this magic stuff than I was, it just made sense for the two guys to get together while Audrey and I went off and amused ourselves.

Because the restaurant was so close, I planned to walk, although I made sure to wear both the protection amulet and the turquoise raven necklace that had once belonged to Mina Powers, as well as the little beaded bracelet of black tourmaline Isaac had given me when we first met. Luckily, the neckline of my sweater was high enough that I could slip the quartz amulet underneath and have only the turquoise visible. Maybe Audrey wouldn't have cared that my look was a little cluttered, but I preferred to keep things simple when I could.

On went the turquoise ring I'd found in Gallup, and I figured I looked ready enough for my little outing.

"You're sure you're okay with this?" I asked Isaac after I descended the stairs. He was sitting in the living room with a book, although, since it lay open in his lap and the spine wasn't visible, I couldn't tell what he'd been reading.

"I'm fine," he said. "After everything that's been going on in your life, I think you've earned a few hours of relaxing and being able to explore a bit. Besides, Michael and I will be close enough... just in case."

He didn't elaborate, but he didn't need to. If a demon decided he didn't care about causing a ruckus in the middle of downtown Santa Fe on a Sunday afternoon, then all I'd have to do was grab the piece of hematite Isaac had given me a while back and send out a call for help.

Also, I was going to be hanging out with Audrey Barrett, a woman who also had her own experiences in facing down demons. She didn't sound as though she was exactly defenseless, either.

So I gave Isaac a kiss goodbye and told him I'd be back in a few hours, and went ahead and let myself out the front door. Not for the first time, I reflected how nice it was to live in a place where I could walk to so many different points of interest and didn't have to get in my SUV every time I wanted to go somewhere.

True, I was just crashing at Isaac's house. It wasn't my permanent home, and neither was my darling rental less than a half mile away. But I had to admit it felt good to be at his place on Del Norte

Lane. I'd only stayed there for two nights so far, but I could already tell we meshed well, that we were both pretty functional in the morning even before we'd had our coffee, that neither of us was the type to take unending showers and hog all the hot water the way my ex used to.

In fact, I thought it seemed pretty likely we'd do just fine living under one roof for an indefinite period, although I had to admit it felt weird to be in separate bedrooms when we clearly had a romantic relationship.

Well, it might be romantic, but it definitely wasn't sexual.

At least, not yet.

I realized I was frowning and did my best to erase the expression as I made my way toward San Francisco Street. The day was really gorgeous—sunny and cool, but not so cold that I felt I needed to put on my coat, which I had tucked under one arm just in case the weather turned cloudy or windy.

It seemed Audrey had been just as anxious to get out as I was, since she'd gotten to the restaurant before me and had already put her name on the waitlist.

"They told me about twenty minutes," she said after we'd exchanged our greetings. "I hope that's okay."

"It's fine," I replied. "Actually, that's really

good for a Sunday. Maybe we beat a lot of the tourists—they tend to come for lunch a little bit later."

"So, you don't regard me as a tourist?" Audrey returned, smiling a little.

A man walking down the sidewalk paused and sent her an admiring glance, but if she noticed, she didn't give any sign of it. Someone that gorgeous was probably used to random men giving her overly appreciative looks.

"No, you're here on business," I said, glad the stranger had apparently picked up on the vibe that she wasn't interested. For just a second, I'd been worried he might be a demon, since they were pretty damn good at assuming a human appearance and hiding in plain sight when they needed to.

But clearly, the man's interest had been based on Audrey's looks and nothing more, and I allowed myself an inner sigh of relief. It would have been really annoying to have our day out interrupted by a demon attack before we'd even had lunch.

Her smile faded a bit. "I guess you could call it that." She sent a quick glance around, probably realizing this wasn't the sort of place where we could go into too much detail about the reasons for hers and Michael's trip to Santa Fe. We were surrounded on all sides by people also waiting for tables, and any conversation on sensitive topics would have to wait.

The gods must have been smiling on us, though, because Audrey's name got called after barely a ten-minute wait, and so we were seated much earlier than either one of us had expected.

I'd already told myself I could have one margarita and no more, just because I knew I needed to be on my toes in case we did encounter any demonic interference. Audrey obviously decided it was okay to follow my lead, because she also asked for one when the waiter came by to take our drink orders.

Once he was gone, I said, "Everything here is good, but some of it can be pretty spicy. Just thought I should warn you."

Audrey sent me a grateful smile. "Thanks for the heads-up. I do okay up to a point, so as long as it's not the sort of thing that's going to make me burst into flames, I should be all right."

"No, it's not quite that bad," I assured her. "It's just that I know everyone has a different tolerance for pain."

Her brown eyes glinted with amusement, but she didn't reply, only went back to the menu, perusing the offerings there. I did the same; I'd been to the restaurant before, of course, but I couldn't claim to have memorized everything on its bill of fare.

When the waiter came back with our drinks, it turned out we'd both settled on chicken enchiladas, making our order easy for him. I raised my margarita on the rocks and said, "Here's to getting out."

"I'll drink to that," Audrey replied, then touched her glass to mine.

A bit later, the waiter arrived with our food, and over the meal, we talked about Santa Fe, about how it was so different from the Southern California Audrey and I both knew well, and about all the stores we'd be able to explore together once we were done eating.

And that was exactly what we did—just went shopping like a couple of regular women who had a few blessedly free hours to wander around and do some serious damage to their credit cards. Or rather, it was Audrey doing most of the damage, since I'd already roamed through downtown with my father a few weeks earlier and had seen most of what was offered. I wasn't the sort of person to amass a large jewelry collection, and nothing really called out to me like the necklace that had once belonged to my mother. In one store, I found a gorgeous embroidered jacket that I decided needed to go home with me, and in another, I splurged on a tooled leather belt with a silver and turquoise buckle, but that was about it.

Whereas Audrey amassed so many bags, I had to help her carry them back to the hotel. Somewhat to my surprise, Michael was already there, apparently done with whatever additional research he'd needed to perform on the sword and the orb. Unlike a lot of other men I knew, he didn't seem too upset by his wife's shopping spree, but only grinned and asked, "Have you thought about how you're going to get all this on the plane?"

She pushed her hair back off her shoulders and smiled at him. "Oh, I'll make it fit," she said, sounding utterly confident.

"So, you're all done at the house?" I said, and Michael nodded.

"I mainly wanted to confirm a few things, and I did. As far as I've been able to tell, the orb is definitely genuine, and the sword appears to have been forged sometime in the seventeenth century. Why then, I'm not sure, although that was a time of a lot of witch trials. Possibly whoever made it intended the blade for self-defense, and it acquired its demon-fighting powers later on. Either way, both artifacts are definitely authentic."

Which I'd already guessed, since otherwise, I doubted they'd be so good at killing demons. Anyway, I told Michael I was glad he'd been able to corroborate his theories and then said goodbye, as I wanted to get back to the house.

After I knocked at the door—Isaac hadn't given me a key...not that I'd expected him to—he answered almost immediately, taking in the two shopping bags I carried.

"That's all?" he said, looking amused by my meager haul.

"Believe me, Audrey did enough shopping for the both of us."

He chuckled and led me into the living room, where the gas fireplace was already going. The book he had been reading earlier now sat on the coffee table with the cover facing up, letting me know it was apparently a volume on herbology.

"Some light reading?" I quipped.

"My mother always told me to never stop learning," he replied, his tone quite serious now. "And so I do my best to follow her advice."

That comment made me just a little ashamed. Oh, I read the odd nonfiction tome from time to time—usually history or true crime—but my previous work schedule hadn't allowed me much room for leisure reading. It certainly wasn't as though I did a lot to improve my mind.

Well, you can pick up War and Peace *once you have this whole demon thing settled,* I told myself. *Your plate's just a little full right now.*

"Audrey seemed to have a good time," I said. "I bumped into Michael at their hotel—he said he'd found what he was looking for, so that seems to be that, right?"

"For now." Isaac settled himself against the back of the sofa, his expression turning thoughtful. "However, it doesn't seem as though he intends to cut their trip short, just in case anything else comes up."

"Like more demon intrusions?" I asked. That was definitely the last thing I wanted to happen, but considering the frequency with which they seemed to cross my path, I thought that sort of incident wasn't entirely unlikely.

"Or anything else along those lines." Isaac shifted just a bit so he faced me more directly, adding, "I wanted to talk to you about tomorrow. I really do need to go into the store—I have one of my first shipments for the holidays arriving in the afternoon, and I need to be there to sign for it. Are you going to be okay being here by yourself?"

"Of course I am," I said at once, even as I found myself wondering whether that was the actual case. Not that I had any problem being alone, but being left on my own in Isaac's house put an entirely new spin on the situation. It would be weird, wouldn't it, to hang out at his place while he was off at work? A thought occurred to me, and I added, "But if you need help dealing with the shipment, I could come to the store with you."

A small smile tugged at one corner of his mouth. "I appreciate the offer, Penny, but I have a cousin who's in high school that I pay to help me with shipments and whatever else needs to get moved around at the shop. He'd be disappointed to miss out on that twenty dollars an hour."

Oh, right. I hadn't realized that Isaac must employ someone, even if on a very casual part-time basis, to manage the parts of the business he couldn't handle on his own, thanks to his physical limitations. And because I really hoped I might become a permanent part of his life, the last thing I wanted to do was piss off a cousin—even a teenage one—by taking away some income he'd been expecting.

"Then never mind," I said hastily. "But really— it's fine. I'll hang out and watch TV or read. Maybe I'll see if Audrey's up for another outing, since it sounds like the two of them are sticking around town for now. Like you said, this house is super safe. And I promise not to clean out your refrigerator."

All this came out quicker than I'd intended, as though by rushing through the words, I could reassure Isaac that everything was just hunky-dory about me hanging out here unattended.

What he was thinking, I couldn't tell for sure, although his mouth had that amused quirk to it which told me he understood all too well how I actually felt about the situation. One hand moved to touch mine as he said, "I know it probably feels a little strange. But I'll come home for lunch, and you know I'll be only about five minutes away. If you start to feel uncomfortable being here by yourself, then come by the shop. It's also a safe place."

Yes, I could believe that. Even if I wasn't into all the metaphysical stuff he sold there, The Enchanted Circle always made me feel somehow calmer, as though Isaac had cast spells to make anyone who entered its doors soothed and focused, ready to find the one item that might make their life a little better.

Or maybe I was simply projecting because that was how Isaac himself made me feel.

"I'm a big girl," I said stoutly. "I'm pretty sure I can hold down the fort until you get home for lunch."

Now he smiled, and reached over and wrapped his fingers around mine. "I know you can. How about we figure out what we want to order in for dinner? I don't feel like cooking today."

That confession didn't surprise me at all. After all his work in the kitchen the day before, I wouldn't be surprised if he didn't want to fix a meal for the next week.

"Sounds like a plan," I said stoutly. "Let's pull up Yelp and see what jumps out at us."

And we turned our attention to his phone while I did my best to ignore any flutters of nervousness at being left alone here the next day. After all, like I'd just told Isaac, I was a big girl.

I could handle this.

Chapter 19
Artistic Bent

That Sunday night was a quiet one. We decided on pizza and salad—there was plenty of chicken molé left over, but neither of us was in the mood for it—ordered from Back Road Pizza, and spent the evening after our meal watching Netflix and snuggling on the couch. Isaac seemed a bit more amorous than the day before... probably because he wasn't exhausted from spending six hours making molé...but once again, our time together ended with a kiss goodnight and both of us heading to our separate rooms.

So much for hoping he might want to have things progress a little further now that he wasn't so tired.

By that point, I was used to disappointment... and used to telling my raging libido it needed to calm down and let matters progress naturally. As I bent over the sink to splash cold water on my face, I had to wonder whether Isaac was doing the same thing, was holding himself back simply because he was embarrassed by his scars or unsure as to how his body might function after so many years of being celibate.

Or maybe he just wasn't that into me and didn't know how to let me down gently.

No, I wouldn't allow myself to believe that horrible thought for a single second. Whatever might be going on inside his head, I could tell from every look, every touch, that he had every intention of keeping me around.

For the thousandth time, I told myself to be patient, and went ahead and climbed into bed.

At least I knew that a good night's sleep cured a whole host of ills.

We were up a little earlier on Monday morning than we'd been the past few days, just because Isaac had told me he always tried to get in to work about a half hour before the shop actually opened, making sure everything was in order and that he had the cash register set up and ready to go at ten. That was fine, because, unlike the previous two evenings I'd spent at his house, I hadn't slept well, had been up and down all night, even though I couldn't say why I was so restless. I couldn't remember having any nightmares, and we hadn't even drunk an entire bottle of wine, but had corked it up after consuming only a glass each.

Well, I'd never been the world's best sleeper, and so I supposed it was inevitable that I would have an uneasy night here eventually. At least I didn't look terribly wrecked, although I applied some concealer under my eyes just to be careful.

Isaac and I shared a quiet breakfast, and then I kissed him goodbye as I sent him on his way. Because he was feeling chipper that day—unlike me—he'd decided to walk to work, something he'd been doing more and more. Honestly, there'd been days here and there where it looked as though he hardly needed the crutches at all, and I had to believe his healing spells were continuing to do their job. At the rate he was going, I really did think he'd be able to move unaided all the time in the not-too-distant future.

After he was gone, I found myself wandering around the house, not sure what I should do with this not entirely welcome free time. Isaac had told me I could avail myself of any of the books on the large shelves in his office, and so I'd gone there first, hoping I might find something that sounded interesting. Nothing really did, but—because I was still fighting with my unruly brain when it came to focus and meditation—I selected a volume on the subject, figuring I should try to make productive use of these hours alone.

Of course, that resolution lasted a whole thirty minutes before I set the book down and tried watching some TV. I'd already noticed that Netflix was the only streaming service Isaac had, although I didn't know that was because he was being frugal and didn't want to spend the money to add any other channels, or whether he simply didn't have much free time for watching television.

Nothing on Netflix really grabbed my fancy, either, and after watching an episode of *The Great British Baking Show,* I got up from the couch and went into the kitchen to pour myself a glass of water. Once there, I stood in front of the sink for a moment, staring moodily out into the now-barren garden and wondering if I was going to be under house arrest like this for the rest of my life, Michael Covenant's encouraging words to the contrary.

Don't be an idiot, I scolded myself. *You're seriously cracking up after being left alone here for a couple of hours? Get a grip.*

And okay, I didn't think I was exactly cracking up, but I knew I needed to get myself together. Maybe this would be my life for only a day or so, or maybe it would go on indefinitely, but it wasn't as though I'd been imprisoned in a Siberian gulag or something.

I took my glass of water with me, returned to

the living room, and forced myself to sit through two more episodes of the baking show. By then, it was twelve-thirty, and Isaac appeared, carrying take-out bags from Tia Maria's, one of our favorite downtown restaurants.

"Ready for a burrito?" he asked.

"You have no idea," I replied. Probably, I was more bored than hungry, but any distraction sounded pretty good right then.

We moved into the dining room and sat down, and he opened one of the bags and handed over a foil-wrapped chicken burrito. Because the food was pretty self-contained, we didn't bother with fetching plates, but went ahead and got right to eating.

"Surviving so far?" he asked after he'd taken a few bites of his shredded beef burrito.

"Oh, sure," I lied.

He didn't say anything, but the glint in his dark eyes told me he could tell I wasn't exactly being truthful. Rather than give me any grief over my prevarication, however, he went on, "It's been busier than usual today. I think people are already gearing up for Christmas shopping."

Which made the shipment he'd be getting that afternoon even more important. "Well, that's good," I said. "The holidays will probably be here before we know it."

And I stopped there, realizing why I'd been

feeling so restless. No, I didn't have regular hours to keep the way Isaac did, but I still had a project I needed to get done by December first. In all the madness, I'd completely forgotten that my story-boards were due in three weeks, and I'd barely gotten started on the job.

"Oh, shit," I blurted out, and Isaac tilted his head at me.

"What's the matter?"

"My storyboard project. Here I've been sitting on my ass, trying to fill up my time, and I had all this work just sitting there, waiting for me." I paused, then added, "I really need to go over to the house to get all my supplies. I can pack some extra clothes while I'm there, too."

At once, his brows drew together. "I'm not sure I like the idea of you going over there alone."

To be fair, I really didn't like it, either. All those demon attacks were enough to make anyone jumpy.

Before I could reply, though, Isaac spoke again.

"Can you wait until I'm off work? Then we could drive over there together."

I supposed I could do that, although, now that I'd remembered how much work I needed to get done, I kind of hated the thought of sitting on my rear end all afternoon when I could be getting at least a couple of storyboards finished.

Then a notion occurred to me. "How about if

I see whether Michael and Audrey can go over there with me? Having them along should be plenty of protection, shouldn't it?"

At once, Isaac's expression cleared. "Yes, that would work—if they're not busy."

Right. Audrey had mentioned that she and Michael had planned to go sightseeing today, although she hadn't said exactly where or when.

"Well, if they're busy, then I'll wait until you're off work," I said. "I can text Audrey after we're done eating and see what she has to say."

"That sounds good."

With a plan of action in place—even if I didn't know whether it would really pan out—I went ahead and ate the rest of my burrito with good appetite. While Isaac was off brushing his teeth and getting ready to head back to the shop, I got out my phone and sent a quick text.

Hi, Audrey, it said. *I have some things I want to get from my house, but Isaac doesn't want me to go by myself. Could you and Michael come with me sometime this afternoon if you have a spare minute?*

Her reply didn't come back immediately. In fact, Isaac was just returning to the dining room, expression inquisitive, when my phone finally pinged.

We're just finishing up lunch now, her message said. *But then we'd planned to go back to the hotel for a bit after that. How about we swing by and get you in about a half hour?*

That would be great, I wrote back. *Thanks so much.*

No problem, she responded. *Glad to help. See you then!*

The matter settled, I put down my phone and looked over at Isaac. "They'll be here in a little bit," I told him.

He came over and gave me a quick kiss, his breath all fresh and minty from the recent tooth-brushing. "I'm glad you were able to work it out. Oh, and you'll need this."

He dug in his pocket and handed over a brass key, obviously the one for the deadbolt on the front door.

I stared up at him, more moved by the gesture than I wanted to admit. True, I couldn't go off and leave the place unlocked—especially with all those valuables in the basement—but at the same time, this felt like a big step to me.

All I said, however, was, "Thanks, Isaac. I'll take good care of it."

He smiled, and brushed his fingers over the hand that held the key. "I know you will. But now I really need to get back to the store."

"It's fine," I said. "You have a good afternoon —I'll see you when you get home."

Another kiss, and he was out the door. I

reflected it was probably a good thing that Audrey and Michael were picking me up, because with Isaac's van also in the garage, I probably would have had a hard time extricating my SUV. Now I could just leave it parked where it was.

I didn't have a lot of tidying-up to do after our quick lunch, but I went and threw away the bags and wrappers from our burritos, then headed upstairs to brush my teeth and freshen up. Since there wasn't any point in turning on the TV, not when I knew my ride would be here soon enough, I picked up the meditation book for something to do while I waited, although for someone who was trying to work on her focus, my concentration was pretty well shot.

However, they arrived right on time. It did feel a little weird to let in a couple of guests when Isaac wasn't even there, but I did my best to hide my awkwardness.

"Thanks so much for doing this," I told Michael and Audrey after they walked into the living room. "I have a storyboard project I really need to be working on, so it's kind of silly for me to be sitting here and twiddling my thumbs when everything's just waiting for me over at my house."

"It's fine," Audrey said at once, and Michael nodded in corroboration of her comment. "Like I said, we were going back to the hotel to regroup anyway. We went to the museum of art this morning and were trying to figure out if we wanted to go to another museum this afternoon or just go exploring, so this gives us a chance to make up our minds."

"That's good to know," I replied, relieved I hadn't interrupted any set-in-stone plans. "Let me get my purse."

I'd left it hanging on one of the dining room chairs, so I hurried over and got the purse, then draped it over my shoulder. After that, all I had to do was lock the door behind me and follow Audrey and Michael out to a silver Chevy Equinox, obviously a rental vehicle.

"Which way?" Michael asked after we'd all gotten in and fastened our seatbelts.

"Go down to Rosario and make a right," I replied. "After that, you'll drive about a half mile and then turn right on Griffin Street."

It seemed those simple directions weren't too daunting, because he didn't ask any questions, only headed in the direction I'd indicated. Soon enough, we were pulling up into the driveway of my rental, where Michael parked directly in front of the garage so we could come and go from the back door. I wondered for a moment how he'd known to do that, and then guessed he probably had a similar setup at his own house in Pasadena.

"Oh, this is so cute!" Audrey exclaimed as she took in the small pueblo-style cottage and its neatly groomed front yard. True, it wasn't as pretty now as it had been I'd first rented it, as the flowers had been gone for weeks and the leaves were all off the weeping willow in the front yard, but the architecture held up even without the window dressing of a fresh green garden.

"Yes, I got really lucky when I found this place," I said. "Or rather, I was lucky I met Isaac, because he's actually the one who found it for me. His sister-in-law works at a property management company here in Santa Fe."

"I'd definitely say you were lucky," Audrey replied with a grin. Her brown eyes were filled with amusement, and I didn't have to think too hard to figure out exactly what kind of luck she was talking about.

We got out of the Equinox and made our way up the back stoop. As I fumbled to get my keys out of my purse, I sent a surreptitious glance around. However, I didn't see any sign of mysterious footsteps or anything that would indicate anyone had been here in my absence—except possibly the gardeners, since the grounds were suspiciously clear of fallen leaves.

While I didn't quite heave a sigh of relief, I had to admit to myself that I was happy to see no one had tried to mess with the place while I was gone. Then again, regular thieves would have been deterred by the security system, and any supernatural intruders wouldn't have found much once they made it inside, since all the really valuable stuff currently resided in Isaac's basement safe.

"Come on in," I said after I'd unlocked the door and disarmed the alarm. Again, a quick glance around told me the place appeared untouched, up to and including the spell candle currently burning on the peninsula.

The candle apparently caught Michael's interest right away, because he headed straight for it and then paused as he gave an approving nod. "This is a strong one," he said.

Something that had been tickling at the back of my brain ever since I'd met Michael Covenant came bubbling up to the surface. "Do you mind if I ask you something?"

"Not at all," he replied, while Audrey paused next to him and gave me an inquiring look.

"About magic," I said. "When I first met Isaac, he told me that magic runs in families and passes through the female line, and so there aren't a lot of male magic workers out there. But you obviously use it, and you made it sound as if this Episcopal priest you know does as well. So...how is that possible?"

An odd expression passed across Michael's face, the look of a guy whose kid had just found out Santa Claus isn't real and was now demanding explanations. "Well," he said, after an obvious hesitation, "I don't know if it's as cut and dried as that."

I planted my hands on my hips. "So...Isaac was wrong?"

"Not exactly." Once again, Michael paused, clearly looking for the right words to answer my question. "It's definitely true that there are more female practitioners of magic than there are male, and it's also true that magic tends to run in families. Isaac was raised in such a family, it sounds like, and so he would have been taught what they knew. But there's a lot more to it than that."

"How so?"

Now he glanced over at Audrey, and she gave him a very small nod of encouragement, as though she knew the explanation might take a while but that she also thought he needed to go ahead with it.

And I was fine with that. We were protected in this house, and, next to Isaac's home, it was probably the safest place in Santa Fe for us to be. Also, Michael and Audrey obviously knew how to handle themselves when it came to the supernatural. I could spare a few minutes to get this particular conundrum cleared up.

"I've traveled a lot, met a lot of psychics and witches and those who don't really want to label themselves but who possess magical abilities of varying levels," he said. "Most of them don't come from witch families, or at least, they don't know if they have any kind of a connection to a family with those sorts of talents. I really think a lot of people can access magic in one form or another, although it's also clear that most people don't have any real reason to try."

"And why's that?" I asked, even though I thought I might already know the answer.

"Because if you don't believe in something, you don't have any reason to try reaching out to use it," Michael replied. Now he was leaning against the tiled counter, posture casual, as though he intended to remain there for some time. "Most people don't believe in magic, so they don't attempt to access it."

"But you did," I countered, and he nodded.

"In a lot of cases, magic comes to the fore when you face a crisis or tragedy of some kind," he said, then looked over at his wife before returning his gaze to me. "The same thing happened to Audrey."

It was on the tip of my tongue to ask exactly what kind of tragedy had made them turn to magic, but then I realized that if Michael had wanted me to know, he would have come out and told me directly. The couple had been nothing but friendly to me, but I realized we were barely more than acquaintances at this point, and not in a position to be sharing confidences...other than the ones that had been necessary to explain why the two of them were uniquely suited to fighting demons.

Maybe one day we'd be real friends, if long-distance ones—I could tell that Audrey and I got along great, and I'd like to spend more time hanging out with her—but in the meantime, I could understand her and Michael's reticence.

And maybe my crisis had been discovering my ex-husband's infidelity, thus removing myself from his negative influence and allowing my *chi* to fly free. God only knows how much longer I might have hung around, doing my best to convince myself that everything was okay, if I hadn't discovered him and my friend Casey together in bed that one fateful afternoon.

"In Will's case, his powers come from faith," Michael went on. "If you asked him, he would deny being a practitioner of magic, and in a lot of ways, he really isn't. He just uses his conviction in the power of good to make an excellent assistant if I need to perform an exorcism."

An exorcism? Seriously?

But then I vaguely recalled that apparently *Project Demon Hunters* had been canceled because of some sort of mishap regarding an exorcism they'd been filming, although I couldn't remember any of the details. Not that an exorcism was exactly relevant to what I'd been dealing with lately, although I assumed my late ex-husband might have had a different opinion on the matter. Seeing that demons were real would have been bad enough, but realizing that the demon in question had been possessing you a moment earlier was definitely enough to send someone over the edge.

In a way, though, I thought Michael's explanation of how magic worked in the general population made a lot more sense than what Isaac had told me. I didn't care how insular a witch family might be; sooner or later, their genes would get mingled with those in the general population, therefore allowing a lot more people than one would have thought to have their own particular subset of powers...even if they didn't actually know they possessed those magical gifts at all.

Not in my case, of course; it was painfully obvious that I'd inherited my magical abilities from my biological mother, along with her red hair and a striking family resemblance. Maybe that's why those powers were so strong—they'd hadn't been diluted very much.

"That all makes sense," I said. The Penny I'd been a couple of months ago might have been irritated with Isaac for giving me such a one-sided view of magic, but I liked to think I'd grown up a bit since then. His experience was very different from Michael's, and so he wouldn't have had any real reason to believe it wasn't the whole truth.

"I'm glad I didn't make a hash of explaining things," Michael replied. "And I don't want you to think that Isaac was wrong. He was only telling you what he knew from personal experience."

"No, I get it," I said quickly. "But I don't want to keep you too much longer—just give me a couple of minutes to get my stuff together. There's some bottled water in the fridge if you need something while we're waiting."

Both Michael and Audrey politely refused my offer of water, so I hurried off to the office to pack up my sketchpads and pencils and erasers. Good thing I'd bought myself a big carrying case at the same time I'd purchased all my supplies, so everything was fairly easy to transport.

Two of my overnight bags were already at Isaac's house, but I had a hard-sided rolling suitcase I'd left behind here, since I hadn't thought I'd need that many clothes for our Gallup trip and so hadn't taken it with me. Now I filled it with a good chunk of my wardrobe, although I left behind both my dresses. Yes, according to both Isaac and Michael, I was perfectly safe wandering around downtown Santa Fe, and yet I got the feeling I probably wouldn't be going out for a fancy dinner any time soon.

When I returned to the kitchen, Michael and Audrey were talking quietly, although I couldn't quite make out what they'd been discussing. Besides, they stopped speaking as soon as I appeared, trundling the suitcase behind me while I had the portfolio case shoved under one arm.

"Here, let me take that," Michael said quickly, and grabbed the case just before it started to slide out from my armpit.

"Thanks," I said. "This should be all I need, since I already have a lot of stuff at Isaac's place."

"Need any help with the suitcase?" Audrey asked, apparently not wanting to be outdone by her husband in the politeness department.

"No, I'm fine," I replied, doing my best to smother a smile. "You head on out to the car, and I'll just lock up here."

The two of them nodded and went out to the back porch, while I paused to set the alarm and then hurried outside before it was fully armed.

A muffled shout from Michael was the first sign of anything wrong. I let go of my suitcase and whirled—only to see three tall, black-haired demons converging on him and Audrey.

Holy shit.

My hand went to my hip, just as it had back in Gallup, but of course the sword wasn't there. No, it was tucked away in Isaac's basement.

But Michael wasn't completely defenseless. His hand went to the breast pocket of the loose black jacket he wore, and he grabbed a bottle from inside and flung it at the nearest demon.

Smoke boiled up from its scaly skin, telling me

the little bottle must have contained holy water. Unfortunately, it didn't seem to stop the creature's advance, because it only brushed at its arm, as though swatting away a biting gnat, and continued toward Michael.

Almost simultaneously, Audrey also pulled a vial of holy water from her purse and lobbed it at the demon closest to where she stood...but her attack had the exact same effect, or lack of effect, depending on how you looked at it.

Heart pounding, I scrabbled inside my purse, frantic fingers searching for the hematite stone Michael had given me. I always kept it in an inner pocket, but right now it seemed to have decided to hide in a fold of the lining at exactly the wrong moment.

Damn it—

Because I'd been scrabbling around inside my purse, I didn't see exactly what happened next. All I knew was that when I looked up, both Michael and Audrey lay crumpled on the driveway next to their rented SUV, with the demons standing guard over them.

Oh, no—

Out of nowhere, a woman appeared at the bottom of the porch steps. Her red hair, nearly the same shade as mine, gleamed in the pale November sun. She stared up at me, a triumphant smile on her full lips.

I gazed back in horror. No, she couldn't possibly look that young, like someone in her late forties or early fifties at the most, and yet a sinking feeling in the pit of my stomach told me exactly who she was.

"Hello, Penny," said my grandmother.

Penny's adventures conclude in *Finding Destiny.*

Also by Christine Pope

LATTES AND LEVITATION

(Cozy Mystery/Paranormal Romance)

Caffeine Before Curses

Muffins After Magic

Pastries and Prophecies (March 2023)

―――――――――

UNEXPECTED MAGIC

(Urban Fantasy/Paranormal Romance)

Found Objects

Finders, Keepers

Lost and Found

Finding Destiny (January 2023)

―――――――――

HEDGEWITCH FOR HIRE

(Cozy Mystery/Paranormal Romance)

Grave Mistake

Social Medium

Household Demons

Perpetual Potion

Jingle Spells

Wandering Monsters

Uninvited Ghosts

Prophet Motive

Ballroom Bits (April 2023)

THE WITCHES OF WHEELER PARK*

(Paranormal Romance)

Storm Born

Thunder Road

Winds of Change

Mind Games

A Wheeler Park Christmas

Blood Ties

Healing Hands

Wishful Thinking

Smoke and Mirrors

MISS PRIMM'S ACADEMY FOR WAYWARD
WITCHES*

(Fantasy/Academy Romance)

Misspelled

Dispelled

Expelled

PROJECT DEMON HUNTERS*

(Paranormal Romance)

Unquiet Souls

Unbound Spirits

Unholy Ground

Unseen Voices

Unmarked Graves

Unbroken Vows

THE DEVIL YOU KNOW*

(Paranormal Romance)

Sympathy for the Devil

Charmed, I'm Sure

A Wing and a Prayer

Wish Upon a Star

THE WITCHES OF CANYON ROAD*

(Paranormal Romance)

Hidden Gifts

Darker Paths

Mysterious Ways

A Canyon Road Christmas

Demon Born

An Ill Wind

Higher Ground

Haunted Hearts

THE WITCHES OF CLEOPATRA HILL*

(Paranormal Romance)

Darkangel

Darknight

Darkmoon

Sympathetic Magic

Protector

Spellbound

A Cleopatra Hill Christmas

Impractical Magic

Strange Magic

The Arrangement

Defender

Bad Blood

Deep Magic

Darktide

THE DJINN WARS*

(Paranormal Romance)

Chosen

Taken

Fallen

Broken

Forsaken

Forbidden

Awoken

Illuminated

Stolen

Forgotten

Driven

Unspoken

THE WATCHERS TRILOGY*

(Paranormal Romance)

Falling Dark

Dead of Night

Rising Dawn

THE SEDONA FILES*

(Paranormal/Science Fiction Romance)

Bad Vibrations

Desert Hearts

Angel Fire

Star Crossed

Falling Angels

Enemy Mine

TALES OF THE LATTER KINGDOMS*

(Fantasy Romance)

All Fall Down

Dragon Rose

Binding Spell

Ashes of Roses

One Thousand Nights

Threads of Gold

The Wolf of Harrow Hall

Moon Dance

The Song of the Thrush

THE GAIAN CONSORTIUM SERIES*

(Science Fiction Romance)

Beast (free prequel novella)

Blood Will Tell

Breath of Life

The Gaia Gambit

The Mandala Maneuver

The Titan Trap

The Zhore Deception

The Refugee Ruse

STANDALONE TITLES

Hearts on Fire (Paranormal Romance)

Taking Dictation (Contemporary Romance)

Golden Heart (Gaslight Fantasy Romance)

Night Music: A Modern Reimagining of The Phantom of the Opera (Contemporary Romance)

Ghost Dance: A Sequel to Gaston Leroux's The Phantom of the Opera (Historical Mystery/Romance)

Flight Before Christmas (Fantasy Romance)

* Indicates a completed series

About the Author

USA Today bestselling author Christine Pope has been writing stories ever since she commandeered her family's Smith-Corona typewriter back in grade school. Her work includes paranormal romance, cozy paranormal mystery, and urban fantasy, among others. She makes her home in New Mexico.

Christine Pope on the Web:
www.christinepope.com

 facebook.com/ChristinePopeAuthor
twitter.com/ChristineJPope

 pinterest.com/ChristineJPope
bookbub.com/authors/christine-pope

Made in United States
North Haven, CT
14 December 2023

45750367R00193